FARGO FIGHTS BACK

"We're gonna kill you, you bastard!" Shep shouted.

"And then we're gonna have some fun with your woman!" another man shouted.

"Well, come and get her, then," Fargo shouted. "There's three of you and only one of me. Or would you like me to turn around so you can shoot me in the back?"

Fargo could hear the men talking amongst themselves. It sounded as if they were arguing.

"Well? What's it going to be? Or are you going to sit here all day?"

No reply.

"You three started this," Fargo called out. "Come on, let's finish it . . . or are you just a bunch of cowards?"

"I'll show you who's a coward," somebody shouted, and Fargo saw a man stand up.

"Shep, damn it—" one of the others shouted, but it was too late.

Fargo pointed his gun from the side of the horse trough and fired once. . . .

THE
TRAILSMAN
#204

THE
LEAVENWORTH
EXPRESS

by

Jon Sharpe

A SIGNET BOOK

SIGNET
Published by the Penguin Group
Penguin Putnam Inc., 375 Hudson Street,
New York, New York 10014, U.S.A.
Penguin Books Ltd, 27 Wrights Lane,
London W8 5TZ, England
Penguin Books Australia Ltd,
Ringwood, Victoria, Australia
Penguin Books Canada Ltd, 10 Alcorn Avenue,
Toronto, Ontario, Canada M4V 3B2
Penguin Books (N.Z.) Ltd, 182-190 Wairau Road,
Auckland 10, New Zealand

Penguin Books Ltd, Registered Offices:
Harmondsworth, Middlesex, England

First published by Signet, an imprint of Dutton NAL,
a member of Penguin Putnam Inc.

First Printing, November, 1998
10 9 8 7 6 5 4 3 2 1

The first chapter of this book originally appeared in *Silver Hooves*,
the two hundred and third volume in this series.

 REGISTERED TRADEMARK—MARCA REGISTRADA

Printed in the United States of America

The Trailsman

Beginnings . . . they bend the tree and they mark the man. Skye Fargo was born when he was eighteen. Terror was his midwife, vengeance his first cry. Killing spawned Skye Fargo, ruthless, cold-blooded murder. Out of the acrid smoke of gunpowder still hanging in the air, he rose, cried out a promise never forgotten.

The Trailsman they began to call him all across the West: searcher, scout, hunter, the man who could see where others only looked, his skills for hire but not his soul, the man who lived each day to the fullest, yet trailed each tomorrow. Skye Fargo, the Trailsman, and the seeker who could take the wildness of a land and the wanting of a woman and make them his own.

April 1859, Kansas Territory—
where the goldfields turned the
hearts of some men black . . .

1

As if it wasn't bad enough being left on foot, he was on foot with a woman along. In town, in the saloon, in bed she was welcome, but out here, where the terrain was flat and hard and he wanted to be able to move fast, she was a hindrance. The only good things about having her along was that they were able to keep each other warm at night. Also, she carried some supplies, but not much. It was left to Fargo to carry his rifle and saddlebags and nothing else. Whatever meager supplies had been on the stage were in a sack carried by Karen, but not without complaint. In fact, all she did all day for the past three days was complain.

"Fargo," she said, "I can't go on."

"Yes, you can."

"I can't," she said. "I'm exhausted."

"We've got to keep moving, Karen."

"What makes you think you're going to catch up to them on foot?"

"I'm not," he said. "What I'm going to do on foot is get to a town where I can get a horse and then catch up to them."

"And then what?"

"And then recover what they stole, and bring them in to hang for killing Zack Wheeler."

Wheeler had been driving the stage when they got into trouble. It was the inaugural run for the fledgling stage line, the Leavenworth and Pikes Peak Express Company. They were going to run between Fort Leavenworth in the Kansas territory to the Kansas goldfields. They had hired Fargo to ride along because part of their first run included the payroll for the mines. They wanted to make sure the first run was a success so that they could continue on from there.

It was Fargo's job to make sure the payroll got to the mines safely, and he still intended to see to it, even though the payroll had taken a short detour.

"Fargo," she whined, "we have to stop."

"No, we don't, Karen," he said. "Not until we reach there."

"Where?"

He pointed ahead of them where, on the horizon, he could make out the silhouette of a town. The sun was going down behind it, and it wasn't much more than shadows right now, but it was a town, he could see that.

"Thank God," Karen said. "Maybe they'll have baths and a bed."

"And a horse," Fargo said, "and a telegraph line."

"Fargo," she said, "you don't intend to take me with you while you track those robbers down, do you?"

"No," he said, "I don't. You can stay here, or try to make your way back to Fort Leavenworth, or you can go on. It doesn't matter to me."

They walked along, drawing closer to the town, and now her silence was petulant rather than complaining.

"It's not my fault," she said finally.

"What isn't?"

"That I'm whiney and crabby. Any woman would be if she was forced to walk for three days."

"I'm sure you're right."

"You shouldn't hold it against me," she said. "You have to admit we had fun in town."

"Yes," he said, "we did—we had a lot of fun in town . . ."

Fargo turned over in bed and stared down at the girl lying next to him. She was on her back, and the bed-sheet was down around her waist. He admired the compact, tight body that he knew from personal experience contained boundless energy. She was young, in her early twenties, and her taut breasts had no sag to them, even though she was lying on her back. Her skin was pale, her nipples rosy in hue, erect even in sleep. Was she dreaming of him? If she was, he was about to make her dreams come true . . . again.

Fargo had arrived in Fort Leavenworth four days earlier and had met the girl, Karen, that evening. She worked in the saloon known only as #5, one of five girls who were serving drinks while the place was open, and making their own way when it closed. That night Fargo brought her back to his hotel room, and she had been coming back every night since. The only difference was, that first night he had paid her.

That first night she had surprised and delighted him with her energy and enthusiasm. In return—according to what she told him afterward—he had made her dreams come true.

"How did I do that?" he'd asked.

"I was dreaming that a man would come to town, a good-looking man who knew how to treat a woman, and that I wouldn't be stuck with some fat, smelly drifter or storekeeper."

"Well then," he'd said, "I was happy to be of service, ma'am."

And he had been "of service" every night since.

Now, on their fourth morning together in Fort Leavenworth, she smiled in her sleep as he leaned over and kissed first one nipple, then the other. He drew them into his mouth, rolled them with his tongue, then sucked as much of them into his mouth as he could. She moaned and stretched, and he withdrew from her so he could watch. He'd learned over the past few mornings that she stretched quite a bit upon waking, and he enjoyed watching her lithe, taut body go through the motions of waking up.

"Good morning," she said, smiling up at him.

"Good morning," he said, and bent to his task again.

She moaned as his mouth roamed over her body, waking her up. He tongued her deep navel, ran his nose through her pubic hair, then touched his tongue to her, tasting her. She caught her breath and wrapped her fingers in his hair, pressing his face to her. She moaned louder and began to grind her firm butt into the sheets as he devoured her.

Without allowing her to ride out the waves of pleasure that were racking her body, he slid atop her and rammed his rigid penis into her. She was wet and hot, and he slid in easily.

"Oooh, my God," she groaned, "ooh, yes, Fargo, yes . . ."

Her orgasm, which she thought was over, seemed to go on and on, and he took her in long, hard strokes. He slid his hands beneath her so he could cup her buttocks and pull her to him each time he drove himself into her. She wrapped her arms and legs around him, raked his back with her nails, and sank her teeth into his shoulder. The bed began to move, but neither of them noticed. They didn't care if anyone below them or on either side could hear them. She began to moan and cry out, and he started to grunt from the effort of screwing her.

"Jesus, yes," she said, urging him on. "Oh, yes, Fargo, harder . . . faster . . . don't stop . . . ooooooh . . ."

She began to buck beneath him as one orgasm ran into another, something she had never before experienced with a man, whether she was sleeping with him for business or pleasure.

"Oooh, God," she said, and then began to beat on his back with her fists, saying, "Stopstopstop!"

"Now you want me to stop?" he asked, puzzled.

"Yes!" she almost shouted. "I want to take you in my mouth."

"I think we can arrange that," he said. He withdrew his throbbing, engorged penis from her. It was slick with her juices and felt cold as the air hit it.

"On your back!" she commanded.

"Hurry," he said. "I'm cold."

"Not for long," she said.

She slithered down between his legs and her tongue ran along his shaft. Then suddenly she opened wide and swooped down on him, and the heat of her mouth closed around him.

"Yesss," he said as she began to suck him, her head bobbing up and down. She kept one hand wrapped around the base of him, while she fondled his testicles with the other, finding tender little spots with her fingertips. She rode him with her mouth, sucking him wetly, greedily, until he felt the rush building up in his legs, flooding toward a release until finally he erupted inside her mouth. She peppered his thighs and crotch with light little butterfly kisses and was shocked to see that he was still hard.

"Not still," he told her, "again."

"You're an amazing man," she said, rubbing her fingers over him, then taking him in her fist and pumping him. She did this, slowly at first, then faster and faster until she once again had him on the verge of an explosion. She released him then, raised herself above him, and sat on him, taking his length deep inside of her.

"Oh, ooh, you're so big, this is . . . glorious," she said as she rode him up and down, her hands pressed down onto his belly for leverage as she rose and fell on him. The bed began to jump again, and it was only later, when they got out of bed, that they realized how much it had moved across the room.

Finally, he was ready again, and he went off inside her. She felt as if there were thousands of tiny hot needles inside her. She closed her eyes, bit her lip, threw her head back, and enjoyed every second, milking him with her wet insides until he was drained dry again. She literally fell off him then and lay beside him, exhausted.

"God," she said, "oh, my God."

"Are you done?" he asked.

She slapped his side and said, "Don't tease me. Even you couldn't get ready again after that . . . could you?"

"You never know," he said, turning toward her, "until you try."

2

It was a town, all right. They came to a sign that said BARLOW, POP. 130.

"Not much of a town, is it?" she asked.

"Big enough to have a bathtub," he said, "and some food."

"Wonderful town," she said, "isn't it?"

They walked until they reached the main street. It was late afternoon, when the main street of any town should have been bustling with activity. Here in Barlow there was no one in sight.

"What's going on?" she asked.

"I don't know. Let's keep walking."

As they continued down the street, he a big broad-shouldered man with weathered clothes and she a rather bedraggled-looking young woman who would be very pretty when cleaned up, Fargo could almost feel the eyes watching them.

"Is it deserted, Fargo?" Karen asked. "Is it a ghost town?"

"No," he said, "there are people here."

"How do you know?"

"Well, for one thing," he said, "I can feel them."

"And for another?"

"There is smoke coming out of a couple of chimneys."

She noticed it, too, then.

"So where are they?"

"They're inside," he said, "watching."

"Are they . . . afraid?"

"That might be it."

"Of us?"

He shrugged.

"Who knows what's gone on here before we arrived?" he asked. "Let's find the hotel—ah, there it is."

They walked to the Barlow House Hotel and entered the lobby. It was clean, not covered with dust the way it would have been had the place been a ghost town.

They walked to the front desk, and Fargo set down his saddlebags and rifle. Karen put down the sack of supplies she was carrying—not much in it, now, after three days—and slumped against the desk.

There was a bell on the desk, and Fargo rang it for service.

"Hello?" he called out.

Nothing.

"Somebody's here," he said, half to himself. "The place is too clean."

Karen reached over and rang the bell again, three times in succession. Finally, someone appeared.

Fargo had left Karen in his bed in his hotel room that morning and walked to the office of the Leavenworth and Pikes Peak Express Company.

The reason Fargo had agreed to take the job with the Express Company to ride shotgun on their first run was because Dave Silver, one of the partners, was a friend of his.

"We'll pay you top dollar," Silver had explained when Fargo arrived in Fort Leavenworth in response to a telegram. "I don't expect you to do this out of friendship."

"It's not the kind of thing I usually do, Dave," Fargo had said, but he took the job anyway.

There had been some problems already, though, which was why he was still in Fort Leavenworth after four days. He wasn't complaining about having to spend four nights with Karen, but he was beginning to get antsy and wanted to get the job under way.

As he entered the office, Silver—a florid-faced man in his forties, whose hair was beginning to match his name—looked up from his desk.

"Did it come in?" Fargo asked.

"Finally!" Silver said. "It's at the bank."

"We were waiting for you to arrive so we could go and get it."

The third man speaking was Silver's partner, Jeff Hodge. He was in his mid-thirties—closer to Fargo's age than to his partner's—and well dressed. He looked more like a gambler than the owner of a stage line.

"What about the sheriff?" Fargo asked.

"He saw the payroll to the bank," Hodge said. "Apparently, it's our responsibility to get it out when we're ready to roll."

"And when will that be?" Fargo asked.

"As soon as we get the money out," Silver said. "Zack is ready to go, and so is the coach."

"What about the passengers?"

"They've been ready," Hodge said.

There were going to be four passengers on this coach for its first run. Three men and a woman—and the woman was Karen. She was ready, she had said, to leave town and head for the goldfields to see if she could earn her fortune. Fargo wasn't quite sure what she intended to do—saloon girl, prostitute, whatever—but he knew she was ready to get going.

"Will you tell them?" Silver asked.

"He can't," Hodge said. "He has to come with us to get the money. Send Zack."

"All right," Silver said. "The men are all at the hotel."

"So is Karen Forbes," Fargo said. "In my room at the moment."

Silver grinned at that, but Hodge frowned. Fargo had already discovered that Hodge had high morals and expected other people to live up to them. With that attitude he was destined to go through life disappointed.

"I'll tell Zack," Silver said. "Wait here for me."

"We won't go to the bank without you."

Silver nodded and left, leaving Fargo alone with Hodge. It had been apparent from the first day that neither man felt comfortable with the other. Hodge thought that Fargo was a cretin, and Fargo thought Hodge was a fanatic. They didn't like each other, and had only one thing in common—Dave Silver.

"I expect you'll be glad to get this coach on the road," Fargo said.

"You have no idea," Hodge said. "This is a bad sign,

having our first coach be late already. We're lucky we didn't lose the passengers."

"That might have something to do with the fact that there's no other coach heading for the goldfields."

"Yes, I realize that," Hodge said, "but still . . . They could have demanded their money back."

"You're lucky then."

"Yes."

They stood that way, in an awkward silence, until Silver returned.

"Okay," he said, "Zack is going to tell the passengers we're ready."

"When did you tell them we'd be leaving?" Hodge asked.

"As soon as they can all get here." He turned to Fargo. "Shall we get the payroll?"

"You fellas lead the way," Fargo said. "It's your show."

The man who came out of the backroom of the Barlow House Hotel looked more like an undertaker than a hotel clerk. He was tall, thin, and pale, with eyes that were so pale in color they almost weren't there. His appearance shocked Karen into complete silence.

"Help ya?" the man asked.

"We need a room."

"Jest one?"

"Two if you have them."

"Got plenty of rooms," the man said. "Don't nobody come to Barlow no more."

Fargo decided not to ask why.

"Want us to register?"

"Don't have no registration book," the man said. "Ain't had one for a long time."

That meant there was no book for Fargo to check for recent guests who might have arrived with a stolen payroll in tow.

The man turned and plucked two room keys from pegs on the wall.

"Here ya go," he said, handing Fargo the two keys.

"Thanks. Do you want to know how long we'll be staying?"

"Don't need to," the clerk said with a shake of his head.

"Do you have a lawman in Barlow?"

"Sure do," the gaunt man said. "Sheriff Fletcher. Office is out the door and to your left. Can't miss it."

"Thanks. Is there anyplace in town I can buy a horse?"

"Livery, I expect."

"W-what about a bath?" Karen asked, finding her voice. "Is there anyplace I can get a bath?"

"Right here, ma'am," the man said. "You jest tell me when, and I'll draw one for ya. Hot or cold?"

"Hot, preferably," she said. "Could you do it in the next fifteen minutes?"

"Do it now if you want, ma'am."

"That'd be fine."

"It'll be ready for ya when ya come down."

"How many tubs do you have?" Fargo asked.

"Jest the one."

"I guess I'll use it after the lady, then."

"That's fine."

"We'll go up and get settled in our rooms, then come back down."

"That's fine."

"Thanks."

Fargo picked up his saddlebags and rifle and started up the stairs with Karen close behind.

"He scared the hell out of me when he appeared," she said in the upstairs hall. "He looks more like an undertaker."

"He's harmless."

"Well, I know that . . . now."

"Here you go," he said as he matched the numbers on the keys with the numbers on the doors. "You take the first one. Mine's across the hall."

He unlocked the door, pushed it open, and handed her the key.

"Will you come with me when I go down for my bath?" she asked.

"Sure," he said. "I'll knock on your door in ten minutes."

"Thanks, Fargo," she said. "After my bath I'm going to have to find something to wear."

When the stage had been robbed, the men had ransacked everyone's bags, looking for more items of value. All Karen's clothes had been torn or tossed in the dirt. All Fargo had on the stage with him was his saddlebags, and those hadn't been touched. He had a clean shirt in there, and not much else.

"We better get some rest before we think about buying new clothes," Fargo said.

"All right."

"And a meal."

"I'm starved," she said. "I hope there's a place to eat in this town."

"There will be," Fargo said. "What they're serving, though, might be another story."

Karen made a face and went into her room.

3

Fargo had walked with Silver and Hodge to the Fort Leavenworth Bank, where the bank manager himself, Henry Wellsworth, waited on them.

"Didn't leave that money in here very long, did you, Dave?" Wellsworth asked.

"We never intended to, Henry," Silver said. "That's earmarked for the miners in the goldfields."

"Of course," Wellsworth said. "I knew that."

The money was brought out in a metal box by a bank guard.

"Do you want the chest, Dave?" Wellsworth asked.

"Put the money in two sacks," Fargo said. "It'll be easier to handle than in that heavy chest."

Wellsworth looked at Silver, who nodded. Fargo noticed that all of the bank manager's remarks were directed at Dave Silver. He seemed to be pointedly ignoring Jeff Hodge and, for that matter, him.

Wellsworth turned to a teller and said, "Transfer the money to two of our bags."

"Yes, sir," the man said.

Wellsworth turned back to Silver.

"I can have my man accompany you to . . . well, wherever you're taking the money."

"Back to our office for now," Silver said, "and then onto the stage—and no, that won't be necessary, Henry. That's why Fargo is here."

"Yes, well," Wellsworth said, casting a quick, skeptical glance at Fargo, "my men are bonded."

Silver laughed.

"I trust Fargo, Henry," he said. "There's nothing to worry about. This is his job."

"If you say so," the bank manager said, but he was obviously unconvinced.

When the money was in two bags, the teller approached, one in each hand, unsure as to whom to hand it.

"Give it to Mr. Fargo, Jenks, there's a good lad."

"Yes, sir."

But Jenks couldn't lift the two bags very high, so Fargo reached over and took them, easily accommodating their weight.

"Thank you for your help, Henry," Hodge said. They were the first words he'd spoken, and that apparently made Wellsworth uncomfortable.

"Yes, well . . ." he said, then looked at Silver. "Anytime I can be of help, Dave."

"I know that, Henry," Silver said. "Thanks."

Outside, Fargo said to Hodge as they were walking behind Silver, "What's his problem?"

"Henry? Thinks he's better than everyone else."

"He seems to like Dave."

Hodge smirked and said, "Everyone likes Dave, didn't you know that?"

Fargo wondered if that was a comment or a complaint.

"He acted like we weren't even there."

"As far as he was concerned," Hodge said, "we weren't."

Fargo thought that a dislike for—or by—the bank manager might be some common ground for him and Hodge, but it wasn't working out that way, so he let it drop.

When they got back to the Express office, Silver opened their safe and put the two money bags in.

"You'll have to stay here with the money, Fargo," he said, closing and locking the door, "while we get the coach ready."

"Like you told the bank manager, Dave," Fargo said. "This is my job."

"Now, you know I consider this more of a favor than a job, Fargo. I was just telling Henry—"

"Hey, that's okay, Dave," Fargo said. "If you're paying me, it's a job. Let me do mine, and you go and do yours. All right?"

"All right," Silver said. "Coming, Jeff?"

"Right behind you, Dave," Hodge said, "as always."

In Barlow Fargo walked Karen downstairs for her bath. When they got there, the tub was steaming.

"I'm going to take a walk, Karen, find the sheriff's office and maybe someplace to eat."

"You're going to leave me here alone?" she asked, eyes wide.

"Like I said, the clerk is harmless."

She gave him a sly look and said, "But you wanted a bath, too. We could share the tub."

As tempting as that was, Fargo decided it was wiser

to decline. Karen had been fun in Fort Leavenworth and a pain in the ass on the road. He decided it was better to move forward and keep his distance.

"I'll be back for you," he said. "When you finish your bath, go back to your room. I shouldn't be long."

He left her there and went back to the front lobby, where the clerk stood behind the desk.

"It's kind of a quiet town, isn't it?" he asked.

"Dying," the man said.

"What?"

"It's a dying town," the clerk repeated. "Dying towns are usually quiet towns."

"Sounds like you've lived in a few."

"My fair share."

"Is there a place to get a decent meal?"

"Depends on what you mean by decent," the man said. "There's one place a block beyond the sheriff's office where you can get a steak."

"Sounds good," Fargo said. "We'll try it. Thanks."

"Sure."

"Oh," Fargo said before he left, "the lady would like some privacy back there. She's probably going to soak for a while. You know how women like their baths."

"You tellin' me not to go back there?"

"That's what I'm telling you."

"Don't have to be told that, mister," the man said. "I ain't no peeper, and I ain't no rapist."

"Those are two goods things not to be," Fargo said, then left.

He turned left outside, walked a block, and saw that the clerk had been right. You couldn't miss the sheriff's office, not when it had a shingle hanging like a doctor's office that said SHERIFF SAMUEL FLETCHER.

Fargo walked in without knocking. He always figured that the town sheriff was a public figure, so his office was a public place. He stopped just inside and closed the door behind him. The office was clean, medium-sized, and empty. The usual trappings were on the walls, including a gun rack with a few empty spaces, like gaps in a person's teeth.

"Hello?" he called out.

Suddenly, a man appeared from the back, where the cells were. He was about forty, a bit disheveled, and he looked surprised.

"Sheriff Fletcher?"

"That's right," the man said, coming out the rest of the way. He looked as if he'd been asleep in a cell. His hair was mussed, his clothing wrinkled, although clean. "You lookin' for me?"

"I am."

The man walked to his desk, scratching his head, then suddenly—as if he realized how he must look—running his hands through his hair.

"I must look like shit," he said self-consciously. "To tell you the truth, nobody hardly looks for me. Ain't much to do around here except take a nap."

"I see."

"And we don't get many strangers," Fletcher said. "Fact is, I didn't hear you ride in."

"I didn't," Fargo said. "We walked in."

"We?"

"There's a woman with me."

"And you're on foot?"

28

"We were on a stage that was robbed," Fargo said. "Only two left alive, actually."

"Where'd that happen?"

"About three days east of here."

"Why'd you walk here?"

"We just started walking, hoping to come to a town."

"Well, you made a mistake, mister," Fletcher said. He was starting to wake up. "Barlow hasn't been a town for some time now."

"But it's here," Fargo said. "You're here, the hotel's here—"

"And not much else."

"Sign says population one hundred and thirty."

Fletcher laughed shortly.

"The sign ain't been updated for a while."

"How many people do live here?"

Fletcher shrugged.

"Forty, maybe a few more."

"You'd notice if strangers rode in, then."

"I didn't notice you."

"I didn't ride, remember?"

"Right. You're wondering if your stage robbers rode in."

"That's right."

"Ain't seen 'em."

"Don't you want to know how many of them there were?" Fargo asked.

"One, two, three, or four—I didn't see any of them," Fletcher said.

"There were four."

Fletcher shrugged.

"Ain't seen 'em."

"The desk clerk said I might be able to buy a horse at the livery."

"Might be," Fletcher said. "We still got one, and there's some horses in it. Plannin' on trackin' those robbers down?"

"That's what I was thinking."

"Well, good luck. What about the woman?"

"What about her?"

"She's going with you, ain't she?"

"I thought she'd stay here."

"That wouldn't be a good idea," Fletcher said. "In fact, where is she now?"

"At the hotel."

"Alone?"

"She was taking a bath."

"And you left her there alone?"

"Why not? The clerk seemed harmless."

"Mister," Fletcher said, "I was you, I'd hightail it back to the hotel."

"Why?" Fletcher was puzzled.

"Because there ain't been any women in this town for months," Fletcher said. "All we got livin' here is men, and if word gets out that there's a woman takin' a bath at the hotel . . ."

"And how would the word get out, Sheriff?"

"Well, Silas—that's the clerk you were talkin' about, except he owns the hotel—he might be harmless, but he ain't above makin' some money any way he can."

"Are you saying—"

"I'm saying," Fletcher repeated, "if I was you, I'd get back to the hotel, pronto."

Fargo started for the door, then stopped.

"Aren't you coming?"

"No," the lawman said. "You look like you can handle yourself. To tell you the truth, I ain't seen a woman in a while, myself. Is she good-lookin'?"

"Very."

Fletcher thought a moment, then said, "Naw, wouldn't exactly trust myself over there. You better hurry along, mister. Silas could be selling off pieces of her by now."

4

"They're in the waiting room," Dave Silver had told Fargo.

"All of them?"

"Except for your girl," Silver said, "and she'll be along."

Fargo walked to the other end of Silver's office. From a small window he could look into the room Silver and Hodge had built for people to wait for the stage.

"Tell me about them."

"You think one of them might be planning something?" Silver asked.

Fargo looked at him, and said, "My job, remember?" then looked back into the room. There were four men there, waiting for the stage to leave.

"Tell me about them."

Silver walked over by him so he could look into the room, too.

"Furthest one from us is Edward Murphy. Apparently he's on his way to open a saloon. See that briefcase he's holding close to his chest?"

"His stake?"

Silver nodded.

"Why doesn't he wear a sign around his neck, 'All my money's in here'?"

The man was well-dressed and groomed, in his mid-forties, short with a bit of a paunch. He'd fold at the first sign of trouble. He was no danger.

"Next," Fargo said.

"The gray-haired man is Mike Gravlin," Silver said. "It's premature, because he's only my age."

"You're starting to show some gray, too."

"Yeah, but I've earned it."

"And he hasn't?"

"I don't know if he has or not," Silver said. "He's some sort of speculator, I think, on his way to see if there's any future for him in the goldfields."

"He looks like he can take care of himself."

"I suppose."

"Next."

"The older man is Judge William P. Server," Silver said.

"Judge?"

"Retired," Silver said.

"Why's he want to go to a gold town?"

"I don't know," Silver said. "I'm not going to get into the habit of asking people why they want to ride our stage, as long as they pay."

"Good point. And the fourth man?"

"His name is Melancon," Silver said. "I think his first name is Carlos. As far as I can see, his business is looking slick."

"That'll serve him well in a gold town. He looks like a gambler."

"He probably is."

33

The man in question looked about thirty, with black hair that gleamed with some kind of oil. He had a carefully trimmed mustache that he was always touching, high, sharp cheekbones, and a strong profile. The women would love him, but men would watch him closely and keep their wives and purses close to them.

"And then there's Karen," Fargo said. "Five passengers in all?"

"That's it."

"And me and Zack."

"And the payroll."

At that moment the office door opened, and Jeff Hodge walked in.

"The stage is ready. Time to get the money on board, then we can bring it around and load the passengers in."

Silver nodded and moved to the safe. He twirled the dial, opened it, and then stepped aside so Fargo could take the bags out.

Fargo reached in, pulled them out, and set them on one of the desks, Silver's.

"What are you doing?" Hodge asked.

"Opening them."

"You were here when we put them in there, and you've been here all along."

"And I was at the bank when they transferred the money from the chest to the bags," Fargo said. "I still want to open them and have a look inside. You have a problem with that?"

"Take it easy, Jeff," Silver said. "This is what we're paying Fargo for, to be careful." He looked at Fargo. "Go on, open them."

Fargo opened both bags, looked inside, reached in, and brought out some of the money.

"Ain't you gonna count it?" Hodge asked.

"Now, that's not my job," Fargo said, putting the stacks of money back in, then closing the bags, which were secured by straps and buckles.

"Satisfied?" Hodge asked. "Did you think one of us was gonna try to steal it?"

"If you were," Fargo said, "there'd be better ways and better places to do it than from your own office."

He grabbed the two bags and slid them off the desk. He managed to carry them both in one hand—his left—leaving his right hand free.

"Let's go," he said.

When Fargo got to the Barlow Hotel, the clerk, Silas, was not at the desk. He could hear voices from the back though. He hurried to the hall and down to the room with the bathtub. The voices were coming from there.

"Ain't that water gettin' cold, missy?" he heard a man ask.

"Go away!" Karen shouted. "If Fargo finds you here, he'll kill you."

"We'll take that chance, missy," another man said. "After all, they's five of us and only one of him. Now come on, you come out of that tub. We're too gentle-men-like to come and git ya."

"You stay away."

"Lonnie," a third man said, "I'll go and get her. I ain't no gentleman."

"Whataya think, miss?" the man called Lonnie asked. "Should we let Shep come and get you?"

"Only if he wants his eyes scratched out," Karen said.

"Whataya think, Shep? Want to take the chance?"

"She's a good-lookin' woman, Lonnie," Shep said. "I'll do it."

At that point Fargo opened the door and walked in. He assessed the situation quickly. There were five men in the room—none of them was Silas—and they formed a semicircle facing the bathtub that Karen was huddled in. All five men turned to face him. One of them started to speak.

"You must be that Fargo she's been goin' on about—" he said, but that was as far as he got. This had to be Lonnie, from the sound of his voice. Fargo drew his gun, stepped forward, and whipped it down onto the man's nose. He turned then and backhanded another man across the eyes. Both of them went down. He turned and pointed the gun at the other three, one of whom was probably Shep.

"Which one of you is Shep?" he asked. "The one who's not a gentleman?"

None of the three men answered. On the floor the other two were moaning. One was bleeding from a gash above his eyes, the other profusely from the nose. Fargo abruptly bent and disarmed both of them. He removed their guns from their holsters and tossed them into the tub with Karen.

"Speak up," Fargo said. "If you don't tell me which one is Shep, I'll just shoot the three of you."

The two he had clubbed looked to be the dangerous

ones. They had both been wearing guns and trail clothes. The other three looked like storekeepers, and only one was wearing a gun.

Two of the men stepped away and pointed to a third.

"That's Shep."

"You sonofabitch—" Shep said to the man.

"Shut up, Shep," Fargo said, cutting him off. Shep was the one wearing a gun. "Take your gun out of your holster with two fingers and toss it into the tub."

"It'll get ruint!" he complained.

"Just do it, and do it without peeking."

Shep reluctantly obeyed and tried to drop the gun into the water without looking. He almost missed, but the gun hit the edge of the porcelain tub and fell into the water with a splash.

"Now come over here by me," Fargo instructed.

"What are ya gonna do?"

"Come over here, or I'll shoot you in the knee. You'll never walk right again."

"Aw, mister, we was just havin' some fun," one of the storekeepers said.

"We didn't mean no harm," the other chimed in.

"Do one of you own a general store?" Fargo asked.

"I do," one of them said.

"I'm going to need some supplies."

"You got 'em," the man said. "Whatever you want, no charge."

"You got any women's clothes?"

"S-some."

"Get out, then."

"Yessir!"

37

The man started for the door in a hurry, but Fargo stopped him.

"Take one of them with you."

The storekeeper bent to the man who was bleeding into his eyes and helped him out the door.

"What can you do for me?" Fargo asked the other man.

"I own the livery."

"Ah!" Fargo said. "I need a horse."

The man swallowed.

"Sure."

"In fact," Fargo said, "I'll probably need two."

"W-whatever you say."

"Okay, then you get out, too, and take him with you," Fargo said, indicating the man who was bleeding from the nose.

"Y-yessir."

The liveryman helped the other man up and then went out the door.

"Now you," Fargo said, "Shep."

"I ain't got nothin'!" Shep said.

"Come over here."

Shep moved forward and stopped arm's length from Fargo.

"Turn toward the tub."

The man did so, his back to Fargo, who saw his shoulders hunch.

"Now apologize to the lady."

"Ma'am," Shep said, "I'm truly sorry—"

Fargo cut him off by clubbing him over the head with his gun. The man dropped like a stone, and Fargo stepped over him. He got a towel and held it out to Karen, who stood up and accepted it.

"See what happens when you leave me alone?"

"Get dried off," Fargo said. "We've got some shopping to do."

5

Fargo, Silver, and Hodge stowed the two moneybags into the stagecoach while Zack Wheeler stood aside and watched. Wheeler was an old-time stagecoach driver, and it tickled him to be in on the birth of a new line. He was in his sixties, but he had forearms and upper arms that had been hardened by years of controlling teams of horses.

"All right," Silver said, "we can finally load the passengers."

Fargo tossed his saddlebags up to Wheeler, who stowed them under the seat, and then the Trailsman climbed up next to the old driver.

"Ever ride shotgun before, son?" Wheeler asked.

"Once or twice."

Wheeler looked around and asked, "Then where's yer shotgun?"

"I'd do better with this," Fargo said, patting his holster.

Wheeler laughed and laughed until he wheezed to a stop just before Fargo expected him to have a heart attack.

"What's so funny?"

"I jest never seed a Shotgun without a shotgun, is all," Wheeler said. "No offense meant."

"None taken."

Wheeler started the team and drove the coach around to the front of the Express office. Silver and Hodge went through the building, and while Hodge waited in the office, Silver informed the passengers it was time to board.

"It damn well is about time," Judge Server complained.

"Yes, sir, Judge," Silver agreed, "it is."

The men had all risen to board the stage and stepped outside when Fargo noticed Karen crossing the street toward them. Not late, but not exactly on time, either. He dropped down to the ground to help her board.

"Gentlemen," he said, stopping the men, "if you don't mind, we'll let the lady board first."

"I'm sure no one minds," Silver said over the grumbling of a couple of the men.

"Not at all," Carlos Melancon spoke up as Karen approached. "It would be my pleasure to assist you aboard, señorita."

Karen gave Fargo what she thought was a secret smile and took the hand Melancon was offering her.

"Thank you kindly, sir," she said, and Fargo wondered idly—and totally without jealousy—if the Mexican had ever been a customer of hers.

Once Karen was aboard, the men climbed aboard, as well, and Dave Silver closed the stage door on the Leavenworth and Pikes Peak Express's first run. He slapped the side of the stage, indicating that everyone was on board, and then waved as Zack Wheeler snapped the reins at the team to get them going.

Fargo turned and saw his friend waving, but did not wave back. There was a lot of money on this stage, and he figured the word must have gotten out somehow. He was going to have to keep his eyes open real wide.

In Barlow, once Karen was dressed, Fargo took her to the general store with him. While he stocked up on supplies, she managed to find something to wear. She bypassed the meager supply of dresses the store had—she said they were hopelessly "outdated"—and simply picked up a couple of pairs of jeans and some shirts.

"I ain't got no ladies' underwear," the storekeeper said apologetically.

"I don't believe I'll be needing any," she said, and oddly, the man blushed.

Fargo had picked up enough supplies to keep them going for a while, but not enough to weigh them down.

"Thanks for your hospitality," he said to the storekeeper, who looked forlorn as his stock went out the door without any money changing hands.

Coming out of the general store, Fargo and Karen ran into Sheriff Fletcher.

"I see you managed everything all right," he said to Fargo. "Is this the lady we were talking about?"

"This is Karen Forbes," Fargo said, making the introductions. "Karen, this is Sheriff Fletcher. He's the one who warned me you might be in trouble."

"Don't judge the boys too harshly, miss," Fletcher said, touching the brim of his hat. "Fact is, they ain't seen a woman as pretty as you in a long time."

"That's no excuse for their behavior, Sheriff," Karen said.

"Of course not."

"They weren't hurt too bad, I hope," Fargo said to Fletcher.

"I wouldn't know," Fletcher said.

"Is there a doctor in town?"

"No," the lawman said. "He was one of the first to leave. Whatever happened between you and whoever was at the hotel, they'll have to care for themselves. Ma'am." He touched his hat again and was on his way.

"Well," Karen said, "he's helpful."

"From what I've been told about this town," Fargo said, "he doesn't get much practice dealing with people."

"What have you been told?"

"That this is pretty much a dying town."

"What about strangers?" she asked. "Has anyone seen any, besides us?"

"No," Fargo said. "In fact, the sheriff didn't even know about us until I told him."

"Fargo," she said, "I'm not staying here when you leave."

"No," he said, "you're not. Come on, we've got to go and buy two horses."

They walked to the livery, where they found one of the men who had been trying to get Karen out of the tub. As they entered, he had the apparent good sense to be embarrassed. Fargo figured now that Karen was out of the tub and dressed, she was more of a person to him, and the man couldn't bring himself to look at her.

"I got some horses out back," he said, and led the way out the back door.

Fargo saw a corral with half a dozen horses in it. None of the animals looked as if they could go a mile without stopping to rest.

"These won't do me any good," Fargo said. "You've got to have something better than this."

"Well . . ." the man said.

"Where?"

The man kicked at the ground a bit before finally answering.

"Inside."

Fargo didn't know if the man had been trying to hide them, but when they went inside, the man showed them three horses in back stalls. All three were healthy, good-looking animals.

Fargo stared at the man, who said, "I . . . I forgot about these."

"Yeah, right," Fargo said. At that point he figured the man was hiding them because he thought he was going to have to "give" Fargo two horses.

"Look, friend," Fargo said, "I just want to buy two horses, all right, not take them from you."

"Oh," the man said, "you want to *buy* them?"

"That's right."

Suddenly, the man became more animated and began singing the praises of the animals.

"That is," Fargo said, interrupting him, "I want to buy them . . . cheap."

"Cheap?"

Although Fargo didn't intend to walk out of there with two horses for nothing, he did intend to make the man pay for harassing Karen, along with the others. Three of them had been clubbed, and the general store owner had paid with supplies. In the end, they walked out of the livery with two horses virtually for the price of one.

"Oh," Fargo said, "and I'll need two rigs."

"Saddles, blankets . . ." the man said.

"Right, canteens, the whole works. We'll work out a price later."

"When do you want all this?"

"First thing in the morning," Fargo said. "Have them saddled and ready to go."

"Yes, sir," the man said glumly.

"Maybe next time," Karen said, just before they left, "you'll think twice about bothering a lady when she's trying to take a bath."

Fargo and Karen left the livery. The next thing on their list was a meal.

"Do you think we let him off too easy?" she asked.

"No," Fargo said. "Those horses would have fetched him a pretty penny. As it is, the person who buys that third one is probably going to have to pay for the deal we got."

They found the place the desk clerk had told him about, and when they entered, they could smell steak frying. Karen's belly made a noise, and she clutched it and looked embarrassed.

"Me, too," Fargo said.

They took a table, and a man came out of the back room—the kitchen—drying his hands on an apron. He was middle-aged, fat, and pleasant-looking.

"Ah, a gentleman and a lady. What can I do for you, please?"

"A couple of those steaks you're frying would be nice," Fargo said, "and maybe some vegetables."

"Best I got," the man said, "but vegetables are scarce around here. I can make some biscuits, though."

"Biscuits sound fine," Fargo said, "and some coffee."

"Coming up," the man said. "It isn't often I get strangers in here to feed."

"So we understand," Fargo said.

"It's a quiet town, isn't it?" Karen asked. She was wondering why this man had not shown up at her bath with the others. Maybe he just hadn't gotten the word.

"Too quiet, miss," the man said. "You have no idea."

The man went back to the kitchen, and Karen looked at Fargo.

"Are you going to start hunting those men tomorrow?" she asked.

"That, and I've got to find a telegraph office to send a message back to Fort Leavenworth and let them know what happened."

"There's something I didn't tell you," she said.

"What's that?"

"I know Jeff Hodge pretty well."

"That's your business."

"My point is," she said, "he's gonna think you took off with the money."

"Dave Silver won't think that."

"You know Silver," she said, "and I know Hodge. That's what he's gonna think."

"Well," Fargo said, "there's one way to prove him wrong, isn't there?"

46

6

"What you lookin' aroun' for?" Zack Wheeler had asked Fargo.

They were only two hours out of Fort Leavenworth, but Fargo was on the alert.

"That's my job, Zack," he said.

"I thought this here payroll was supposed to be a secret." Wheeler said. "You expectin' somebody to try somethin'?"

"I don't think it ended up as much of a secret as it started out," Fargo said. "Once the whole thing was late in getting rolling, it must have gotten out what the holdup was."

"And what was it?"

"We were waiting for the money to get here."

Wheeler spat some tobacco juice into the wind, which Fargo deftly avoided with a jerk of his head. He heard a wet splat behind him as the glob landed on somebody's luggage.

"Well, see, I didn't know that," the old man said. "I didn't know nothin' about no money until Mr. Silver told me about it las' night."

"Well, that's good," Fargo said. "At least it was that much of a secret."

Abruptly, Wheeler reined the team in and brought the coach to a stop.

"What's wrong?" Fargo asked.

"I don't like the action on one of the horses," Wheeler said. "I'm gonna check. You might as well drop down and check on the passengers."

Fargo was immediately suspicious. Was Wheeler lying when he said he knew nothing about the money? Was this part of the setup to give someone a chance to hold up the stage?

Wheeler dropped down and walked over to the horses. Fargo took the time to look around. There wasn't much cover, and he didn't see anyone lurking nearby. If Wheeler was going to stop them someplace where a holdup could take place, this wouldn't be it.

As Fargo was climbing down, he heard the judge complain loudly, "Why are we stopping?"

Fargo walked to the coach and opened the door. First he exchanged a smile with Karen and then directed himself at the men in the coach.

"How is everyone doing?"

"We'd be fine if we could just get under way," the judge said. "What are we stopping for? We're barely out of Fort Leavenworth."

"The driver is just checking on the horses," Fargo said. "We should be moving shortly, if everything is okay with them."

"Your company should have made sure you had healthy horses hitched to this thing," Edward Murphy complained. He was clutching his little briefcase to his chest as if he thought Fargo was going to try and take it away from him. Idly, Fargo wondered what the man would do if he did.

"One of the horses could have picked up a stone bruise along the way, Mr. Murphy," Fargo said. "Or stepped in a chuckhole. We'll know soon enough."

"But—"

Fargo was finished talking with them, though. He closed the door and walked to the front of the coach, where Wheeler was still examining the horses.

"How do they look?"

"One of them picked up a sliver of something," Wheeler said.

"Is he hurt?"

"Naw," Wheeler said, straightening up and brushing dirt from his hands. "It was just enough to make him uncomfortable. We can get moving now."

"Fine," Fargo said, "let's do it, then. I don't like sitting still for too long."

"I don't blame ya."

Fargo watched as the old man nimbly climbed back onto the coach. He admired the way the man moved at his age.

"We're getting ready to roll again, folks!" he shouted up and climbed up alongside the old man. He took a moment to lean over and check on the money-bags.

"All there?"

"The bags are there," Fargo said.

"Couldn't nobody get to them lessen they was a magician," Wheeler said.

"I'm just checking, Zack," Fargo said, "doing my job."

"Let's get movin' then," Wheeler said. He snapped the reins at the horses, and they started forward.

"What do you think of our passengers?" he asked.

"What about them?"

"Well, the judge there is a crotchety old bastard, and that Murphy fella sure does have somethin' in that briefcase that he's proud of."

"I noticed."

"Pretty gal, though, huh?" Wheeler said, leering. "Bet you noticed her, too."

"Yeah, I did."

"And she noticed you, too," Wheeler said. "Big young buck like you probably has plenty of women, huh?"

"I'm sure you do all right in that department, Zack," Fargo said.

"Oh, sure," Wheeler said, "I get me some women sometimes, only I got to pay for 'em. Bet you don't, huh?"

"Sometimes I do," Fargo said, "and sometimes I don't."

He caught the old man staring at him.

"Better keep your eyes on the road, Wheeler."

"These horses ain't gonna run off a cliff or nothin'," the old man said.

"Maybe not," Fargo said, "but I don't like being stared at."

Wheeler cackled and looked away.

"Didn't mean no harm," he said, cackling. "Jest lookin', is all. Jest lookin'."

* * *

If Barlow was dead during the day, it was worse during the night, more like a graveyard than a town.

"I don't even see how they can say there's forty people here," Karen said.

They were in Fargo's hotel room, and she was looking out the window. They'd decided it would be safer for Karen to stay in Fargo's room with him.

"You'd think somebody would be moving around down there."

"Let's just assume that someone is," Fargo said. He was lying on his back on the bed with his hands behind his head. He was still wearing his gunbelt.

She turned and looked at him.

"You're not expecting trouble from that storekeeper and the liveryman, are you?"

"Not from them."

"The other three? I thought you scared them out of their wits."

"Maybe they're scared," Fargo said, "and it would be much better if they were, but I wouldn't let a man do to me what I did to them and get away with it."

"Well," Karen said, walking to the bed, "they're not the man you are, are they?"

She knelt down by the bed and ran her hand over his chest.

"What are you doing?"

"What else is there to do here?" she asked, sliding her hand down to his crotch. "Besides, having all those men in the room while I was naked in the bathtub kind of got me excited."

"Excited?" he asked. "You didn't look excited when I came in."

51

"Well, maybe not then," she said, "but after. You know, there I was naked, and helpless, with five men in the room—some women dream about situations like that, then wake up and call it a nightmare—but they're breathing hard. Do you know what I mean?"

She undid his belt.

"Have you ever awakened from a dream breathing hard?" she asked, unbuttoning his pants.

"Once or twice," he said, "but it was usually because somebody was chasing me in my dream."

"Men," she asked, "or women?"

She reached in and freed him from his underwear. His penis was hard, and she stroked it.

"If it was women," he said, "I wouldn't be running, would I?"

"No," she said, "not you. Lift your hips."

He did as he was told. She undid the gunbelt and slid it from beneath him.

"Hang it right there on the bedpost," he said, "where I can get to it."

"Are you gonna shoot me if I don't satisfy you?" she asked, doing as he told her.

"I don't think that's going to be a problem," he said. "Do you?"

"Definitely not. Lift your hips again."

He did so and she slid his pants and underwear down to his ankles. His erection sprang out as if it had a life of its own, and she smiled.

"Ah," she said, "there's my friend."

"Hey," he said, "how about getting rid of my boots so I can kick off these pants and shorts."

"Do you feel trapped?" she asked, reaching for him and stroking him.

"Well, trapped is not the word," he said, "but I can't spread my legs."

She leaned over him and pressed her face to his belly. Her mouth was warm on his skin, her tongue wet. He shifted his legs but they were encumbered by the pants and underwear around his ankles.

She continued to lick him until she reached his penis. She used those butterfly kisses on him again, this time all over his thighs and hips, all around his penis but never on it, causing it to fill with blood and become more and more engorged.

She shifted position so that she was on the bed with him, placed one hand on each of his thighs, and bent over him. She kissed his penis, and then opened her mouth and took him inside. He tensed, lifting his hips to the pressure of her mouth as she suckled him.

"Mmmmm," she moaned sliding one hand beneath him to cup his heavy balls, hefting them, fondling them.

Abruptly, she released him and stood up from the bed.

"What are you doing?" he asked.

She didn't answer. Instead, she removed all her own clothing and stood naked before him. His eyes roamed over her. She had a truly lovely, athletic body, all taut and smooth, and well muscled. She got on the bed with him again, straddled him, rubbed her hands over his chest and belly.

"Karen, come on . . ."

"What?"

"Free my feet."

"You free them," she said, laughing.

Before he could move she mounted him, sliding down over him, taking him all the way inside until she was sitting down tightly on him. She began to ride him, and he forgot about his legs. He ran his hands up her ribs to her small, firm breasts, then pulled her to him so he could reach the nipples. She laughed, then moaned, and held his face to her breasts as she continued to move her hips. He moved with her, finding her cadence and matching it. Eventually, he let himself fall back onto the bed, and she sat up straight on him, sliding up and down his slick shaft, faster and faster, groaning, crying out until finally he couldn't hold it in anymore. He exploded inside her, lifting his butt off the bed, lifting both of them up, and he emptied into her.

7

It had happened so quickly that Fargo didn't have a chance to react. He'd have to think about it again later to really understand what occurred.

One moment he was sitting next to Zack Wheeler on the coach, and the next he was flying through the air. His arms and legs windmilled, but there was no way to control or direct his fall. He finally hit the ground hard, all of the air driven from his body. As he lay there, gasping for air, thinking it would never come, he heard the shots, and the shouts of people—frightened people, angry people.

"No, hey, no, this wasn't—" he heard, thinking it was Zack Wheeler, and then there was another shot.

Suddenly, he was able to take a breath, as if a band of leather around his chest had suddenly released. He took the air in, held it, savoring it, then released it and took in another one.

"Come on, come on!" someone said urgently. "We gotta get movin'!"

Painfully, Fargo rolled over onto his side, and took in another breath. He tried to look around, but he was disoriented. He grabbed for his gun, but it wasn't there. It must have fallen out of his holster either when he was flying through the air or when he landed.

"Come on, gimme one of the bags!" The same voice, still filled with urgency. "Take the other one."

"I got it."

"Are they dead?"

"It sure looks like it."

"Then let's go!"

As he struggled to rise even to a seated position, he heard the horses riding away, a lot of horses, maybe half a dozen or more. He tried harder and got to his feet, swaying but standing. He wiped a hand across his eyes, trying to clear them, but he was dizzy. He crouched, hands on his knees, until the dizziness passed, then straightened and took his first good look around.

He could see the coach, without horses. On the ground next to it was Zack Wheeler. Fargo went to the old man and bent painfully over him, but there was nothing he could do. The driver was dead.

He looked at the rig that had held the horses to the coach and saw that the leather straps had been cut. That was why he'd heard so many horses, because the four in the team had been driven off.

Suddenly, he climbed halfway up onto the coach and felt around beneath the seat. The moneybags were gone, of course. That was what they were after. Also strewn about the coach, on the ground, were the contents of the passengers' baggage. Apparently, the robbers had looked for anything of value they could get their hands on.

Fargo's next thought was of the passengers. He

went to the door of the coach, which was not only open but had been half torn from the body of the coach. He looked inside and all he could see was blood. The robbers had simply pumped a barrage of bullets into the coach, taking care of the passengers.

Including Karen.

That was when he heard the moan, a sound made by a woman.

"Karen?"

"Fargo? What happened? Hey, I can't move!"

That was because she had a dead man lying on top of her. Fargo entered the coach and pulled the body of the judge off her.

"Are you all right?" he asked.

"I-I think so. What happened?"

"Apparently, when the first bullet hit the judge he fell over on you, shielding you."

"I hit my head," she said. "I remember. The coach hit something and lurched, and I hit my head."

"And I was thrown clear," he said. "Come on, let's get you out of here."

She suddenly became aware of the contents of the coach.

"Oh, God," she said, "are they all dead?"

"Yes, they are. Come on."

He got her out of the coach and away from it. When she saw Zack Wheeler's body, she covered her mouth with her hands.

"Karen, take a minute to check yourself over. Make sure you're not injured."

"What are you going to do?"

"Find my gun."

He walked over to where he had been lying and found the weapon a few feet away. When he came back to Karen, she was feeling her arms, and then her head.

"I have a bump," she said, "but that seems to be it."

"You're lucky the judge's body protected you from the bullets."

"Why didn't they check to see if I was dead?" she asked. "Or you?"

"The killing was secondary," he said. "They wanted the payroll and anything else of value."

"My things!" she said suddenly, looking around.

"Did you have some valuables?"

"No, but everything I own is all over the place."

"Forget it," he said. "We have to travel light, anyway."

"Travel . . . where? How?"

"We'll have to walk."

"Walk? How far?"

"I don't know, Karen," Fargo said. "As far as the next town."

"I . . . why don't we stay here and wait for someone to come along?"

"Because that could take a long time," he said. "Remember, this is a new stage route. We have to get going before they get too far."

"Too far? What are you talking—you're going after them?"

"Well, of course," he said. "It was my job to protect that money, and I didn't do a very good job, did I?"

"Why don't you leave it to the law?"

"Because I can't. Sit down somewhere and wait. I'm going to collect some things from the coach to take with us."

"I thought you wanted to travel light."

"I do. I just want my rifle, my saddlebags, and whatever supplies Wheeler might have had."

He went through the coach and found some beef jerky, some coffee, and a bottle of whiskey, all of which he put into a sack. He walked over to Karen and sat down next to her, handing her the sack.

"I'll carry my things," he said. "You carry this."

It wasn't heavy so she didn't complain—then.

"Fargo, I don't think it's a good idea to go walking away from here. Somebody could come along any minute."

"Or any day," he said, "or week. We can't wait that long, Karen. Come on, on your feet."

"Fargo—"

He took her by the elbow, stood up, and pulled her up with him.

That was when they had started to walk.

Fargo turned away from the window, away from Barlow's main street, and looked at Karen, who was lying in bed with the sheet on her. It molded itself to the taut contours of her body. Fargo was naked, but totally unself-conscious.

"What is it?" she asked, sensing that he had something on his mind.

"I've been going through it all in my head, bringing it all back so I could examine it."

"And?"

"Did you hear anything at all during the robbery?" he asked.

"I heard somebody yell when we hit that bump."

"That must have been me when I got thrown off the coach," Fargo said. "Anything else?"

"Shots, but I think I blacked out when I hit my head. I'm sorry. What did you hear?"

He told her everything he heard, and then repeated something.

"It was Zack Wheeler," Fargo said. "It sounded like he was begging for his life, and then he said something like 'This wasn't—'"

"Wasn't what?" Karen asked.

"I think he was going to say, 'This wasn't the way it was supposed to happen,' or something like that."

"So you think he was in on the robbery?"

"He had to be," Fargo said. "He was too good a driver, too experienced, to have hit that bump the way he did by accident. I think he did it on purpose to take me out of play."

"Well," Karen said, "if he did, he saved your life."

"That probably wasn't on his mind when he did it," Fargo said. "What's more important was he took me out of it, and the robbery went down without a hitch."

"Did you ever think that they might have killed you, too?"

"To be honest," he said, "that never occurred to me."

"No," she said, "it wouldn't."

Fargo looked outside again. It was dark, but he really wasn't trying to see anything on the street. He was still looking inward.

"So how do we find out who Wheeler was working with?" Karen asked.

"I think the first thing we have to find out is who hired him," Fargo said. "Silver or Hodge."

"You don't think one of the partners was in on it, do you?"

"Why not?" he asked. "There was a lot of money in those bags."

"How much?"

Fargo turned and said, "I don't know exactly. It wasn't part of my job to know how much there was."

"How much do you think there was?"

He shrugged. "Fifty, sixty thousand, maybe more . . . maybe less . . ."

"Well, more or less, that's still a lot of money," she agreed.

"A big temptation."

"But if one of them was going to steal it, why would they hire you?"

"Well, if it's Hodge who did it, he didn't know Silver was hiring me. In fact, he was pretty upset when I arrived, and never did treat me decently."

"So it's him."

"But maybe Silver hired me so that when the money was stolen he could *say* he hired me, and therefore couldn't have done it."

"Then it's him."

"Not necessarily."

"Fargo," she said, "come back to bed. You're making my head spin."

Fargo did go back to bed, and Karen cuddled up to him and went to sleep. He closed his eyes as well. He wouldn't ever tell her, but he was making his own head spin.

8

Fargo was entirely in the present when he woke up. Replaying everything in his mind might have helped, but not much. Even if Zack Wheeler was in on the robbery and had been double-crossed and killed, it didn't help him at the moment.

He woke Karen early, and they dressed and went to the livery for their horses. The liveryman—whose name Fargo never got—had both horses ready as promised. In truth, he was too afraid of Fargo to have done anything else.

"What about breakfast?" she asked.

"We can try that cafe again," he said. "The steaks weren't bad yesterday, but if he's not open, we're going to ride."

"I'll keep my fingers crossed."

It worked. The cafe was open, so they tied off their horses and went inside to eat.

The same man served them breakfast, but looked nervous while doing it. His hands shook when he brought out the plates of eggs and ham and when he poured the coffee. Karen didn't notice, but the Trailsman did.

When breakfast was done, Karen started to get up.

"Karen, wait."

"What is it?"

He walked to another table, abruptly overturned it, and then looked at her.

"Get behind this."

"What?"

"Come on," he said, "Crouch down behind here."

"What for?"

"Because we have a problem, that's why."

"What problem?"

"I think when we walk through that door we're walking into an ambush."

She looked at the door, then at him.

"Those men from yesterday?"

"I'm not sure," he said, "but who else could it be?"

"What makes you think—"

"Come on," he said, taking her by the arm and pulling her behind the table. He pushed her down onto her knees, and then turned to the door.

"Wait, wait," she said, grabbing his arm. "Tell me how you know."

"It's just a feeling," he said. "I want to play it safe."

"Well, then, if we're going to play it safe, let's go out the back."

"That's not playing it safe," he said, "that's running."

"What's wrong with running?"

"Nothing, if there's a point. If these men want me, they'll probably chase us. You'll be in danger. It's better to settle it now."

"So you're gonna walk out there and go against three guns?"

"Do you know another way to settle it?"

"This is silly," she said, standing up. He put his hands on her shoulders and forced her down again. "What makes you think there's even anyone out there?"

"The waiter's hands were shaking when he served us," Fargo said. "He's nervous. He's heard something. There aren't that many people in town, and word probably got around."

"Then go to the sheriff."

"That still means we'd have to walk out that door," Fargo said, "and to tell you the truth, I don't think the sheriff would be much help in this situation."

"Skye—"

"Believe me, Karen," he said, cutting her off, "I know what I'm doing. I've been in this situation many times before."

"Men wanting to kill you?"

"Yes."

"Well, fine," she said, sitting on the floor and folding her arms like a petulant child. "Then I won't have to feel guilty that you got yourself killed because of me, will I?"

"No," he said, "you won't. No matter what happens, keep your head down until the shooting stops. Understand?"

"I understand."

Fargo started for the door, but stopped just short of it. He turned and walked to the kitchen. As he suspected, the man who had served them both days was the only person there. As Fargo entered the kitchen, the man tensed.

"What do you know?" he asked.

"About wha—"

"Don't play games with me, friend," Fargo said. "You're as nervous as a cat. Were you afraid they'd start shooting while you were in the line of fire? What do you know?"

"It's just . . . what I heard."

"Which is?"

"That they were gonna try to kill you today before you leave town."

"How'd they know I'd come here?"

"It's the only place to get breakfast this early."

"And you don't know anything for certain?"

"No," he said, shaking his head. "I swear. It's just what I heard."

"All right," Fargo said. "Stay in here, out of the line of fire."

"Yes, sir."

Fargo left the kitchen. He looked over at the overturned table Karen was crouching behind and couldn't see her. Should he take the time to put her in the kitchen? No, better to get outside now, before the men got impatient and started firing into the restaurant through the windows.

As he approached the door, he wondered if the sheriff had heard what the cook/waiter had heard, and if so, where was he this morning?

He walked to the door and stopped just short again to look outside. He used the windows on either side of the door to try to see if anyone was in sight. If they were there, they were behind cover, which meant they had no qualms about bushwhacking him. Leave it to him, he thought, to ride into a town with only thirty or forty people in it, and incite three men to want to kill him.

Then again, there were *only* men in this town, and given the nature of most men in the West, someone would have found a reason to try him. Even with those who didn't know who he was at first, who weren't attracted by the lure of his reputation, they were still drawn to his presence, his attitude, his *confidence*, and they took it as a challenge to their own manhood. He didn't know why men felt that killing another man added to their lives, to their own glory.

He checked the loads in his gun, reholstered it, and stepped out the door.

His senses were immediately alert. It was quiet, the street empty. If he was lucky, he'd be able to hear some telltale sound like . . . that one.

A click! The hammer being pulled back on a gun.

He moved quickly, and it was only his instinct that saved him from that first treacherous shot. He didn't know it at the time, but he had also saved Karen's life. The shot missed him and thudded right into the chair she had been sitting in during breakfast. Crouched behind the table as she was, she was safe.

Other shots followed, and even as he was diving for cover, his eyes were at work, picking them out, finding their cover, counting their number. As he rolled behind a nearby horse trough, he knew that there were three of them, and he knew where they were. Now if his luck continued to hold, the horses wouldn't be hit by any flying lead.

Lying behind the trough, he realized that if he had

been more alert this morning he might have also noticed some nervousness in the desk clerk when they checked out, and in the liveryman when they picked up the horses. Of course, to be fair to himself, they both had reason to be nervous around him anyway.

"Is that you, Lonnie? Shep?"

No answer.

"You boys aren't mad at me, are you?"

After a moment a voice called out, "You busted my nose!" It was sort of muffled.

"Well, you asked for that, didn't you?" He didn't say a name because he wasn't sure whose nose he had busted. All he knew for sure was that he'd hit Shep on the head.

"How's your head, Shep?"

"We're gonna kill you, you bastard!" Shep shouted.

"And then we're gonna have some fun with your woman!" another man shouted.

"Well, come and get her then," Fargo shouted. "There's three of you and only one of me. Or would you like me to turn around so you can shoot me in the back?"

Fargo could hear the men talking among themselves. It sounded as if they were arguing.

"Well? What's it going to be? Are we going to sit here all day?"

No reply.

"You three started this," Fargo called out. "Come on, let's finish it . . . or are you just a bunch of cowards?"

"I'll show you who's a coward," somebody shouted, and Fargo saw a man stand up.

"Shep, damn it—" one of the others shouted, but it was too late.

Fargo pointed his gun from the side of the horse trough and fired once. The bullet struck Shep in the forehead and drove him back through a store window.

Glass cascaded from the window, reflecting the sunlight in a blinding display that Fargo took full advantage of. He stood up and ran across the street, figuring—hoping—that the other two would have been watching Shep go through the window and then might even be caught up in the flashing sunlight as it reflected off the shattered glass.

"Jesus," he heard one of them say, and then he was on the boardwalk, looking at them.

One of them saw him and cried, "Shit."

"What?" the other one said, looking around.

"Hey, wait—" the first man said, but the second man—Lonnie—brought his gun around, trying for a shot. He never made it. Fargo fired once, putting a slug in the man's belly. He dropped his gun and flopped over on his stomach.

"Wait, wait!" the other man shouted frantically. He had a bandage over his eyes, where Fargo had raked him with his gun. He threw his gun away and put up his hands.

"I'm unarmed."

"I should kill you anyway, you bushwhacking bastard," Fargo said.

"No, no, it was Lonnie's idea, Lonnie and Shep, and you already killed them."

"And you just went along for the ride?"

"That's right, that's right," the man said. He was

sweating profusely, and Fargo could smell the fear coming off him in waves.

"Get out of here," he said in disgust. "If I ever see you again, I'll kill you without a word, do you understand?"

"Sure, sure," the man said, scrambling to his feet, "I understand. Thanks, mister."

"Go!" Fargo shouted, and the man turned and ran.

Fargo checked the other two to make certain they were dead, then turned and went back across the street. He checked the two horses to make sure they were unharmed, then went inside to do the same with Karen.

"Is it over?" she asked, looking up at him from behind the overturned table.

"It's over."

"Did you kill them?"

"Two of them," he said. "I let the third run away."

"Why? Why didn't you kill him?"

"He tossed his gun away," Fargo said. "Besides, he can tell the rest of the town what happened."

He helped her to her feet. She looked at the front of the table and saw two spots where bullets had chewed into it. Luckily, the table was thick enough that they hadn't gone all the way through.

"Jesus," she said, "you were right."

"Yeah," Fargo said, "I was."

He ejected the spent shells from his gun, replaced them, and holstered the weapon.

"Are you ready to go?" he asked.

"More than ready, Fargo," she said. "More than ready."

9

They mounted up and rode out of Barlow. When they were a few miles out of town, Fargo reined his horse in and dismounted.

"What are you doing?"

"Back at the stagecoach, after the robbery, I took a good look at the ground."

"Why?"

"I wanted to remember the tracks that were left by the horses those robbers had."

"Aren't they all the same?"

"Not at all," he said, abandoning his search of the ground. He looked up at her. "We followed some of those tracks to Barlow, Karen."

"But . . . I thought we were just walking aimlessly."

"No," Fargo said, "there were tracks." He didn't want to tell her that she was too busy complaining and whining to listen to him talk about tracks. He'd kept quiet about them, and followed them.

"And they led into town?"

"No, not into town," Fargo said. "The sheriff was right about one thing. There were no strangers in town before us."

"But you just said the tracks led to town."

"They led up to the edge of town, but they went around," Fargo said. "We went into town because there were things we needed."

"And now?"

"And now I've got to pick up that trail again."

"Won't it be old?"

"Days old," he said, "still readable." He mounted up and pointed. "They skirted the town to the west of it and kept heading south. All I have to do is pick up the trail again."

"I thought we were riding to a bigger town, one with a telegraph office."

"Oh, we'll be stopping at a bigger town, all right," he said, "and so will they. We'll let them lead us right to it."

Skye Fargo wasn't called the Trailsman for nothing. Eventually, he found the trail left by the stage robbers as they skirted Barlow.

"What makes you think they even know where they're going?" Karen asked.

"Well, for one thing, it doesn't matter if they know," Fargo answered, mounting up again. "What matters is that I pick up their trail and stay with it, and I have."

They started riding again, Fargo keeping his eyes on the ground.

"However, I do think they know where they're going," he continued, "because they knew enough about Barlow to avoid it."

"Do you still think somebody in the company has something to do with it?"

"The more I think about it, the more convinced I

am that Zack Wheeler was part of the plan. What he didn't know is that he wasn't part of the big plan."

"What if it's Dave Silver, Skye?" she asked.

"I hope it's not."

"What if it is? What will you do then?"

"The same thing I'd do if it turns out to be Jeff Hodge," he said, "or even someone else."

"You'd turn in your friend?"

"A friend who tries to use me to steal is not my friend," he said.

"But . . . he's stealing his own money, isn't he?"

"No," Fargo said, "he's only transporting the money to pay the miners."

"But he'd have to make good on the loss, wouldn't he?" she asked. "I mean, whoever was involved, the company will have to make good."

"If they can."

"And if they can't?"

"Then they go out of business."

"So, if one of the partners is involved, he's ruining the other one."

"Right."

"But aren't they friends?"

"I don't know, Karen," Fargo said. "All I know is that they're partners. I don't know if they were friends before, or if they became friends after. I'll say one thing I did notice, though."

"What's that?"

"Silver's the one people react to," he said, "the one they liked, and I don't think that sat very well with Hodge." He looked at her. "You knew him. Do you agree?"

She took a deep breath and said, "Yes. Jeff could be . . . abrasive. He wasn't good with people. At first he seemed glad that Silver was, but later I think he resented it."

"Do you know if they were good friends?"

"No," she said. "Jeff didn't talk much when he was with me."

They rode in silence for a while, and then she asked, "Tell me what you see when you look at the ground."

"Are you really interested?"

"Yes."

"Well, for one thing," he said, "there are four of them. The horses are well shod, seem to be of a kind, except for one. Three of them are long-striding, one is shorter—but the horse with the shorter stride belongs to the leader."

"How do you know that?"

"He's always in front," Fargo said. "In a band like this, where there's a leader, he always likes to ride up front."

"How do you know these things?"

"I've made it my business to know," he said. "It's a result of long years of experience."

"But how do you know these are the same tracks as from the coach?"

He reined in and said, "I'll show you. Get down."

She dismounted and followed him. He went to one knee and pointed.

"What do you see?"

She looked and shrugged.

"Tracks."

"Made by what?"

74

"Horses."

"Look closer."

She did, narrowing her eyes.

"I can't—"

"Look inside the tracks."

She tried again, harder, and then she caught her breath.

"There's a mark . . . inside that track." She pointed.

"Good," he said, "you see it, a little crescent-shaped indentation in the horse's hoof. Probably from an old injury. It doesn't bother him because it's healed, but it makes his track very distinctive."

"I never would have seen it if you hadn't made me look closer," she said. "You look that closely all the time?"

"I do," he said, "at everything."

"Everything?" she asked, touching her face.

"Everything," he said. "Come on. Let's get mounted and move on."

They rode for half a day, and then Fargo announced it was time to camp.

"It's still daylight," Karen said. "Are you stopping for me?"

As matter of fact, he had noticed that Karen was a little sore from riding all day. She obviously knew how to ride, but it was just as obvious that she had not ridden this long in a while and it was beginning to tell on her. To her credit she had done none of the whining she'd done while they were walking.

"No," he said, "although I can imagine how your butt must feel right now. The reason I'm stopping is because I don't have my own horse beneath me, so I don't know how much I can push this one—or yours, for that matter. By the end of tomorrow I should have a better idea."

Fargo knew the horses had to be unsaddled and cared for, and a fire had to be built. He didn't know which of these chores to give to Karen. As if reading his mind, she solved the problem.

"If you'll take care of the horses, I can build a fire and start dinner."

"All right," he said. "Thanks."

"You were thinking about that, weren't you?" she asked. "Wondering what I can and can't do?"

"As a matter of fact, I was."

"Well, you'll find I'm not quite so helpless as you might think," she said, and walked off to collect the makings of a fire.

By the time he had taken care of the horses, he could smell the coffee and the bacon. When he reached her, Karen had an impressive fire going, and she handed him a cup of coffee as he hunkered down by it.

"I did a lot of riding as a child," she said. "My mother died when I was young, and my father liked to travel. He was a gambler. As soon as I was old enough to sit a horse, he took me on the trail. I haven't done it in a while, but it all comes back to you."

"I can see that."

She handed him a plate of bacon and beans, made one for herself, and they sat back and started to eat.

"I have to apologize to you," she said.

"For what?"

"For all the trouble I gave you while we were walking," she said. "I know that by the time we reached Barlow you didn't like me much."

"Well—"

"Don't deny it," she said. "I was a whining bitch the whole way."

"Yeah," he said, "you were."

"It was just all so . . . abrupt, you know?" she said. "I expected a nice smooth stage ride, and look what we ended up with. Everybody else dead and us on foot."

He didn't respond, just let her talk it out.

"I always hated walking," she said. "Even as a child, I could take riding miles, but not walking. I'm afraid I reverted a bit to that complaining child, and I'm sorry for it."

"It's all right."

They ate in silence for a while before she spoke again.

"What do you suppose they're thinking back in Fort Leavenworth?" she asked. "I mean, surely they know by now that the payroll didn't get where it was going."

"I don't know what they're thinking," he said. "Let's suppose that neither of the partners is involved. If that's the case, then Silver is probably worried—about us and the money—and Hodge is probably just worried about the money."

"I'd be surprised if he wasn't all over the sheriff to get a posse together and go out looking for us."

"He wouldn't have much luck there," Fargo said. "The sheriff in Fort Leavenworth wouldn't have any jurisdiction. He'd need to get a federal marshal involved before anything could be done . . . legally."

"What do you mean, legally? How else could something be done?"

"Well, he could simply hire someone to come and find us."

"By someone you mean . . . what? Bounty hunters?"

"Bounty hunters, private contractors, whatever you want to call them. Maybe some detectives."

"Bounty hunters would shoot first and ask questions later," she said.

"Some do."

"We could end up dead before we have a chance to explain what happened."

"Well," he said, "maybe by the time anyone finds us we'll have found the robbers and gotten the money back."

"Do you really think that?" she asked. "That we're gonna find them?"

"I'm going to track them and find them," he said. "Whether or not they still have all the money is another question."

"And if they don't, where will it be?" she asked. "They couldn't possibly have spent that much money in this short a time, could they?"

"Probably not," he said, "but they might split up somewhere along the way, with each taking his share with him."

"Oh, no."

"What?"

"I know what you're going to say next."

"What's that?"

"If that happens you'll track them one by one, won't you?"

"That's very good," he said.

"I think," she said, "I'm starting to know the way you think."

After they finished eating, Fargo rolled out a blanket for each of them. Karen pulled the blankets nearer together so they could sleep closer.

"You don't mind, do you?"

"Not at all."

"Do we need to stand watch?"

"No," he said. "Nobody's chasing us. We're doing the chasing."

"Good."

They got down on the blankets together, and she put her head on his shoulder. He made sure she was sleeping on his left side so his gun hand was free. Maybe nobody was chasing them, but that didn't mean that he could afford not to be careful.

10

They woke in the morning from an uneventful night.
This time Fargo built the fire, but it was still Karen
who prepared the coffee. Fargo decided that coffee
would be enough to start the day, and Karen didn't
argue.

They saddled their own horses and got under way
again.

"Stop," Fargo said around midday.

"Do you want to camp?"

"No," Fargo said, dismounting. "One of the horses
has split from the other three."

"Why would they do that?"

"I don't know."

"Which one left the others?"

"That's the problem," Fargo said. "It's the one with
the nick in its hoof."

"So what do we do now?" she asked. "Follow that
one, or the other three?"

"I believe that the horse with the nick is the smaller
animal."

"And you think that one is being ridden by the
leader, right?"

"Right."

"So would he take the money with him?"

"I don't think the others would like that," Fargo said, "unless . . ."

"Unless what?"

"Well, two things come to mind," he said. "Either they trust him that much."

"Or?"

"Or they were never supposed to get the money in the first place."

"Explain that."

"Maybe the four of them were hired to steal it," Fargo said, "in which case the money has to be delivered somewhere."

"And what do they get out of it?"

"They get paid."

"Enough to convince them not to just keep it once they had it?"

"Either that," Fargo said, "or they're too afraid to keep it."

"Of whom?"

"Either the man who paid then," Fargo said, "or the man who led them."

"So then the leader is taking the money to whoever hired him."

"If I'm right."

"Well, his is still the most distinctive trail to follow, right?"

"Right."

"Is it possible you could lose the others somewhere along the way?"

"Anything is possible."

"Maybe I could follow the one with the nick—"

"I don't think so, Karen."

"Why not?"

"It'd be too dangerous."

"I don't have to do anything once I catch up," she said. "I could simply send a telegram—"

"No," Fargo said, cutting her off. "We'll stay together on this."

"Okay, then," she said, "whom do we follow, the one or the three?"

Fargo thought a moment, then said, "The one."

He mounted up and looked at her.

"When we catch up, he can tell us where he plans to meet the other three."

"That is, if you're right and he has the money," she said. "What if they just had a falling out and the other three drove him away, but kept the money."

"If that happened," Fargo said, "he'd probably double back and try to take the money from them. That's what I would do."

"And that would lead us back to him, anyway," she said. "It sounds to me like you can't lose. You've got it figured every way."

"I never like to think that, Karen."

"Why not?"

"Because somebody always comes up with a new wrinkle just when you think you've got everything smoothed out."

They followed the distinctive trail to a town called Carmody. It was much larger than Barlow, and as they drove down the main street, it was alive with activity.

"Now this," Karen said, "is what I call a town."

"You can stay here if you like," Fargo said.

"But if your man's here, you won't be going on," she said. "Not for a while, anyway."

"This may not be where he's meeting his employer," Fargo said. "It might just be a rest stop."

"Well, we'll know that pretty quick, won't we?" she asked. "After we check the hotels?"

"And rooming houses," Fargo said. "We'll have to stay the night, in any case. It'll be dark soon." He looked at her. "You'll have some time to think over what you want to do."

They rode to the livery. The area out front of the stable was so trampled down that there was no way for Fargo to tell if the distinctive hoofprint was present. The only way to tell that would be to check every horse in the stable.

"Help ya?" the liveryman asked, appearing from inside the stable.

"We'd like to put our horses up for the night," Fargo said.

"No problem," the man said. "I got room."

"No other strangers in town?" Fargo asked, dismounting.

"Plenty of 'em," the man said, "but I still got room. I can take 'em in."

"If you don't mind, we'd rather do that," Fargo said. "They're new mounts, and we're trying to get to know them."

"Pick two empty stalls then, and take care of 'em yerself," the man said. "You'll still have ta pay the goin' rate."

"Not a problem," Fargo said.

He walked his mount into the stable with Karen following.

"Why are we taking care of our own horses?" she asked. "I'm kind of hungry."

"We'll eat soon enough," he said. "I've got to take a look at all the horses in this stable to see if the one we've been following is here."

So while Karen unsaddled their horses and saw to their needs, Fargo went around from stall to stall inspecting the hooves of every horse in the livery. When he finished, Karen had just finished giving their horses their feed.

"Well," he said, "you do know what you're doing, don't you?"

"I told you," she said, slapping her hands together to dispel dust and dirt, "it comes back to you. Any luck?"

"No," he said, "the horse isn't here."

"So he's not in town," she said. "He bypassed this one, too."

"It's the smart thing to do after a robbery," Fargo said. "Don't go into a town until you really need to."

"But he thinks everyone was dead."

"That means we're dealing with a cautious man. Now that you've fed the horses, let's go see about getting us fed, as well."

After they checked in at a hotel, they went to a cafe nearby. They ordered steaks, and as it turned out, even though they were in a larger town than before, the steaks they'd had in Barlow were better.

"It's that personal touch," she said. "This is a bigger place. They don't care as much about their customers."

"Mmm."

"What's wrong? Is your meat worse than mine?"

"Hmmm? Oh, no, I was just thinking."

"About our robbers?"

"About them," he said, "about you. It might be a good idea if you stayed here when I leave tomorrow."

"I've been thinking about that, too."

"So you agree?"

"No," she said, "I don't."

"Karen—"

"I can help you, Skye," she said, "even if it's just building a fire and cooking."

"I can do that. I'm worried that you'll end up getting hurt."

"I can take care of myself."

"Can you?"

"I told you," she said. "I'm not that whiner anymore."

"I wasn't referring to that."

"I can shoot."

"How well?"

"I can hit what I aim at," she said, and then added, "or come pretty close."

"Do you mind if I ask you something?"

"Go ahead."

"How did you end up doing what you do?"

"I rebelled."

"Against what?"

"My father had me riding and shooting at a young age," she said. "When I got old enough I didn't want to do those things. They were for boys, and then men. I wanted to do what ladies do."

He looked at her.

"Okay," she relented, "what *women* do. So I'm not a lady."

"What did you intend to do when you got to the gold fields?"

"I don't know," she said. "Get some kind of job, I suppose. My days of being a saloon girl and a prostitute are over."

"Well, there are plenty of other jobs to be had," he said. "In fact, in a town this size—"

"If you refuse to take me with you, Skye, I'll stay here," Karen said, "but I'd rather come along."

"Karen," he said, leaning forward, "if I took you and you got hurt—or worse—there's no way I'd be able to justify that to myself."

"I see. Then you *are* forcing me to stay."

"Yes."

"I could follow you, you know."

"That would just be foolish."

"You're right," she said. "It would be."

"I'll cover the hotel bill long enough for you to figure out what you want to do."

"I'll have to figure it out fast," she said. "All my money was in my bag, so those stage robbers took it along with the payroll."

"Well then, I'll just have to try and get it back, too, won't I?"

11

After they finished eating, Karen went back to the room while Fargo went in search of the town telegraph office. He had to send a telegram to Fort Leavenworth just in case they were getting ready to send a posse out after him. He addressed the telegram directly to Dave Silver, rather than to the Express office. He didn't wait for a reply. In his message he assured Silver that he'd be tracking down the men who robbed the stage and he'd get the money back.

After that he went to talk to the local sheriff. There was still a possibility that the man he was looking for had stopped in town for a short time, even if he hadn't stayed there. He hoped the sheriff of Carmody was better at his job than the sheriff of Barlow had been.

When he entered the office, he didn't find the sheriff, but he did talk to a deputy named Lang.

"Sheriff Kitchener lives in a house at the south end of town with his wife and kids," Lang said. "He'll be in the office later on. Is there something I can help you with?"

Deputy Lang appeared to be about twenty-five, and was very eager.

"I was just wondering if there had been any strangers in town recently."

Lang peered at Fargo suspiciously and asked, "Are you a bounty hunter?"

"No," Fargo said, "my name is Skye Fargo."

"I know that name," Lang said, frowning. "Is there paper out on you?"

"I don't think my name and face have ever been on a wanted poster," Fargo said. Could Leavenworth have gotten one out so soon? And if they could, would they?

"I've got it," Lang said. "By golly, you're the Trailsman, aren't you?"

"That's right."

"So what brings you to Carmody?"

"I'm looking for a man."

"What'd he do?"

"Held up a stagecoach and killed five people."

Lang whistled soundlessly.

"Where'd this happen?"

Fargo told him.

"Out of our jurisdiction. You were on that stage?"

"I was riding shotgun," he said, then explained the situation to the young man.

"The sheriff will probably want to talk to you, Mr. Fargo."

"Well, I'm at the hotel, and I won't be leaving until morning."

"When he gets in, I'll tell him the story, and he'll probably come over to see you."

"That's fine," Fargo said. "I'll either be there or at the saloon."

"We have a couple of saloons in town," Lang said, "but he'll find you."

"Thanks, Deputy."

"Don't mention it," the young man said. "Just doin' my job, is all."

Fargo left the sheriff's office and decided to go to one of those two saloons rather than go back to the hotel. Karen was still very disappointed, and he didn't want to be around her right now. Not that he was going to change his mind about taking her along, but he didn't want to give her a chance to try to persuade him otherwise.

Fargo was in the saloon maybe thirty minutes when the three hard cases walked in. These men were different from the ones who had tried to bushwhack him in Barlow. The way they moved and wore their guns, they had the look of professionals. Now the question was, exactly what profession, and were they there for him? If they were, several scenarios were possible. Someone had recognized him on the street, and it hadn't taken long for the word to spread.

Either that or the deputy had a mighty big mouth.

Fargo concentrated on his beer and watched the three men in the big mirror behind the bar.

" 'Nother beer?" the bartender asked.

"Sure," Fargo said, "and maybe you can answer a question for me."

"If I can."

"Who are those three fellas who just walked in?"

"Those three," the barman said in disgust. "You

don't want to know those three, friend. They're bad news."

"What do they do?"

"They cause trouble, that's what they do. They cause trouble and they hurt people."

"They live in town?"

"Just outside of town."

"From the way you're talking, it sounds like the sheriff allows them to ride roughshod over everyone. Why does he do that?"

"The sheriff's a good man, mister," the bartender said, "but he's only one man."

"I thought he had a deputy."

"He does," the man said. "Johnny Lang. You see the bigger of the three men there?"

"I saw him."

He had walked in first and had the look of a leader, as the other two remained just behind him to either side.

"Well, that's Danny Lang."

"Father?"

"Not that close," the man said. "Cousin."

"And the other two?"

"His brothers," the man said. "The Lang brothers are related to the deputy."

"I don't get it," Fargo said. "Why would the sheriff hire him?"

"Johnny used to run with his cousins, but he broke away from them. The sheriff thought that pinning a badge on him might do something to keep the Lang boys in line."

"And did it?"

"Not much. Say, you didn't have a run-in with them, did you?"

"No."

"You're not planning to, are you?"

"Well," Fargo said, "I never *plan* on finding trouble."

"Always seems to find you, though, huh?"

Fargo sighed.

"Seems that way."

"Well," the man said, "I'll just go and get you that beer. Maybe you can drink it and then . . ."

"I know," Fargo said, "take my trouble outside."

"I'd appreciate it," the man said. "I own this place, and I'm still trying to make my payments. I can't afford a lot of breakage."

"I'll keep that in mind."

"Appreciate it."

Fargo didn't know why, but he felt that the men were there for him, even though they had managed not to look at him at all during the short time they were there. Or maybe that was why he knew it. When he walked into a saloon, he gave every man there at least one look. So far, these three had not looked his way—and Fargo knew he was the kind of man people looked at twice, men and women.

He didn't nurse his beer, but drank it at a reasonable pace. When he was done, he figured to go back to the hotel and talk to Karen for a while, maybe ease her mind about being left behind.

To get to the door he had to walk past the three men, who were standing at the bar. As he passed them, an odd thing happened. One of them turned quickly, holding a mug of beer, and Fargo knew that the man was going to dump the beer on him—only it didn't happen that way. Instead, the man allowed Fargo to bump his arm, causing him to dump the beer on himself.

"Hey!"

Oh, Fargo thought.

"Why'n't you watch where ya goin'?"

Fargo played his part.

"I was watching where I was going," he said. "You bumped into me."

"Oh," the man said to his two friends, "I bumped into him, he says. You boys saw it. Who bumped into who?"

"He bumped into you—"

"Let me cut this short," Fargo said. "You boys are the Lang brothers, aren't you?"

They all frowned, and the one with beer down his chest said, "That's right."

"And you're Danny Lang, right?" Fargo asked the spokesman.

"Yeah," Lang said, "you heard of us?"

"Oh, yeah," Fargo said, "I've heard of you."

"We don't know you," one of the other brothers said.

"No, I guess you don't know me by name," Fargo said. "Whoever sent you over here to hassle me didn't tell you, huh?"

"No, he did—"

"Shut up!" Danny said.

"Who was it?" Fargo asked. "Your cousin Johnny?"

"You know a lot for a stranger, mister," Danny Lang said. "Who are you, anyway?"

"My name is Skye Fargo."

"Wait a minute . . ." the third brother said. "The Trailsman?"

"That's right," Fargo said. "Johnny didn't tell you, huh?"

"No," the third brother said, looking at his older brother Danny, "he didn't."

"He just described you," Danny said.

"And you were supposed to . . . what? Hassle me? Get me to leave town? Hurt me?"

"Oh, no, Mr. Fargo," the third brother said, "we wasn't gonna hurt you."

"Just scare you a little," the second brother said.

Fargo looked at Danny, who was in charge—sort of.

"How are we going to do this, Danny?" he asked. "One at a time or all at once."

Danny studied Fargo for a moment, then looked at his brothers. "I think all at once we can take him."

"Not without somebody besides me getting hurt," Fargo told them.

"What's Johnny think he's doin', Danny?" the second brother asked. "Sendin' us after the Trailsman without tellin' us?"

"Yeah," the third man said, "is he tryin' to get us killed?"

"Maybe," Fargo said, "you should ask Johnny."

"Maybe we should," Danny said.

"Not until after I talk to him."

Danny narrowed his eyes.

"You ain't gonna kill him, are ya?"

"No," Fargo said, "I just want to talk to him, find out why he sent you after me."

"We was wonderin' that, too," the third brother said. "Why's he got a beef with you?"

"I don't think he does," Fargo said. "I think he was acting for someone else."

"Who?" Danny asked.

"I don't know," Fargo said, "but I'm going to find out. You boys stay out of my way until I do, huh?"

"Sure, Mr. Fargo, sure," the third brother said.

"We'll stay out of your way," the second man said, "won't we, Danny?"

"Yeah," Danny said, annoyed, "sure." Fargo didn't know if Danny was annoyed with his brothers for not backing him, or with Johnny Lang for putting him in this situation.

"Why don't you boys have another beer," Fargo said, "on me."

He stepped to the bar, dropped some money on it, and left the saloon.

If Johnny Lang sent his cousins to scare Fargo out of town, it was pretty obvious that he never told the sheriff about Fargo. Fargo had two ways to go. Find Lang and ask him what was going on, or find the sheriff, tell him what had happened, and then the two of them could find out what it was all about.

He decided on the second way and went in search of the sheriff.

12

The man who answered the door was tall, dark-haired, and fit-looking, with intelligent blue eyes. He would have been handsome if not for an oversized nose that almost looked like a small potato in the middle of his face.

"Can I help you?"

"Are you Sheriff Kitchener?"

"If this is about business, you'll have to talk to my deputy," Kitchener said, annoyed. "I'm having dinner with my family."

"I'm sorry to interrupt your dinner, Sheriff, but the problem is I already talked with your deputy and I didn't like the outcome."

"And what was the outcome?"

"He sent his three cousins after me."

"Damn him!" Kitchener said. Fargo had not expected to be believed so readily. In fact, Kitchener's next question surprised him, as well.

"Did you hurt any of them?"

"Did I . . . no, I didn't hurt any of them."

"What happened?"

"I talked them out of whatever they had planned."

"How did you do that?"

"By telling them my name."

"Which is?"

"Skye Fargo."

Sheriff Kitchener stared at Fargo for a few moments, then backed up and said, "Come in, Mr. Fargo. Would you like a cup of coffee?"

"Sure," Fargo said, "I could use a cup," and stepped into the house.

What further surprised Fargo was that the sheriff introduced him to his wife, Molly, and his two sons, Jason and Willy.

"I'll take the boys upstairs now," Mrs. Kitchener said, after pouring them each a cup of coffee, "and you can have your talk."

"Thanks, sweetie."

Molly Kitchener tossed her husband a smile, said, "Nice to have met you, Mr. Fargo," and shooed the children out.

"Handsome woman," Fargo said, because she was, "and good-looking kids," because that was true, too.

"Thank you. Now suppose you tell me about this conversation you had with my deputy."

Fargo did, and enjoyed the coffee along the way. Mrs. Kitchener made a fine cup.

The sheriff listened intently to Fargo's story of his meeting with the deputy, and his near run-in with the Lang brothers.

"I've seen Johnny since then," he said, when Fargo finished his story. "He didn't tell me a thing about talking to you."

"I guess he just decided to handle me himself."

"What is there to handle?" Kitchener asked. "There was no reason to want you out of town."

"He had to have had a reason, Sheriff," Fargo said. "I figure to ask him, but I wanted to talk to you first."

"I appreciate that, Fargo," Kitchener said. "Why don't you finish your coffee, and we'll both go and ask him, hmm?"

"Sounds good to me."

Lang was sitting at his desk in the sheriff's office when Fargo walked in, with Sheriff Kitchener right behind him. Lang's face twitched, but he did a good job of hiding his feelings.

"Hello, Al," he said to the sheriff. "Finish dinner already?"

"No, Johnny," Kitchener said, "my dinner got interrupted by Mr. Fargo here."

"Who?"

"This is Skye Fargo," the sheriff said, "otherwise known as the Trailsman."

"Nice to meet you," Johnny Lang said, putting his hand out. Fargo ignored it.

"Not very friendly, is he?" Lang asked.

"You and Fargo haven't met before, Johnny?" Kitchener asked.

"No, sir," Lang said. "Why?"

"He says you have met."

"We have?" Lang asked, looking past the sheriff at Fargo. "Well, maybe I just don't remember it. When was this meeting supposed to have taken place?"

"Earlier today."

Lang laughed, as if very amused.

"Well, I think I'd remember that," he said. "I don't know what's going on, Sheriff."

"He says that after you met, and he explained the reason he was here, you said you'd let me know. Then he says he went to the saloon, where your three cousins tried to start a fight with him."

"Did they?" Lang looked at Fargo again, who was rather surprised at the young man's cool demeanor. "I've told them over and over . . . I'm really sorry, Mister . . . what was your name again?"

"I think that's pushing it a bit, don't you, Sheriff?" Fargo asked.

"Yeah, actually, I agree," Kitchener said. "Johnny, I've told you about lying to me—"

"I'm not lying, Sheriff," Lang insisted. "Why would you take his word over mine?"

"Because he's got no reason to lie," Kitchener said. "He's got nothing to gain that I can see. Also, if I go to the saloon, I'm sure there will be witnesses to the altercation with your crazy cousins."

"Hey," Lang said, "all that means is that my cousins started up with him. I've got nothin' ta—to do with that."

"Don't you?" Kitchener asked. "How about if I get Danny and the other boys in here and ask them? Do you think they'd lie to me?"

"In a minute, Sheriff," Lang said, "you know that. Them boys is—are born liars."

Fargo then realized what had been bothering him about Johnny Lang all along. His speech pattern was very mannered, and now that he was under stress he seemed to be reverting to the way he usually spoke.

"Johnny," Kitchener said, "I want your badge."

The younger man looked stricken. "W-what?"

"Your badge," Kitchener said, "let me have it."

"You . . . you can't!" Lang said. "You . . . you cain't . . . uh, can't take my badge, Sheriff."

"Yes, I can, Johnny," the sheriff said. "You've lied to me for the last time."

"Sheriff," Lang said desperately, "you know this badge is the onlyiest—only thing that keeps me from bein' like my . . . my cousins!"

"You should have thought of that before you started lying, Johnny," Kitchener said. "I need a deputy who's going to honor that badge, not try to use it for his own good. Now give it to me, and get out of here. I've given you enough chances."

Lang stared furiously at the sheriff, and then at Fargo. His face was almost bright red as he unpinned the badge and dropped it to the floor at the sheriff's feet. He then stomped on it and stalked to the door. There he turned for one last tirade.

"You ain't heard the last of this, Fargo!" he said. "I'll get you for this!"

"Johnny," Kitchener said, holding the misshapen badge in his hand now, "you're a fool. This man will kill you before you can bat an eye."

"He will, huh?" Lang said. "We'll jest see about that!"

He stormed out the door, slamming it behind him.

"Seems like I cost you a deputy, Sheriff," Fargo said. "I'm sorry."

"It's not your doing," Kitchener said, "it's Johnny's. He thinks he doesn't want to be like his cousins, but it's in his blood. Even wearing a badge couldn't change that. I guess it's just time for me to give up on him."

"Any other prospects for a deputy?"

"You want the job?"

"Not me."

"Then I guess I'll have to try to find somebody who won't mind wearing a bent-up star."

Kitchener walked around behind his desk and sat down.

"I would have liked to find out why Johnny did what he did."

"Well, I guess that's up to you," Kitchener said. "My concern was that he did it, not why. Do you think he's connected with the man you're looking for?"

"I'm going to have to find out before I leave."

"If you go after Johnny, you're going to have to face the other three, too. They'll follow him."

"Isn't he the youngest of the four?"

"Yes, but he's also the smartest. You were able to talk them out of something earlier today, but if Johnny's with them next time, it won't be so easy."

"I guess I'll have to take that chance. He might have some information I need."

"You told me you rode in with a woman. Does Johnny know about her?"

"I didn't tell him."

"He could have found out very easily," Kitchener said. "I wouldn't leave her alone, Fargo, and I wouldn't think about leaving her behind after you leave."

Somehow, that didn't surprise Fargo. He had the

feeling that somehow, some way, Karen was going to end up staying with him.

Of course, if he happened to kill all the Langs, she wouldn't be in danger, but he had no intention of doing that. He just wanted to talk to Johnny, away from the others, and he was going to have to figure out a way to do that.

"So I guess you don't know anything about any strangers coming in to town, Sheriff?"

"I'm not aware of any in the past week, Fargo," Kitchener said. "But if you're right, and someone did ride in and manage to convince Johnny to help him, then I guess I haven't been doing my job any better than Johnny was."

"Don't be too hard on yourself," Fargo said. "It's a tough job."

"One that I used to pride myself on," Kitchener said. "I guess I've been slipping and didn't notice. I should thank you for that."

"I'll be leaving town in the morning, Sheriff."

"Something tells me," Kitchener said, "you won't be staying out of trouble until then."

13

Fargo went back to the hotel to explain the situation to Karen.

"So now you want me to go with you?"

"It's for your own safety," Fargo said, "but the final decision is up to you."

They were in her room, and she was standing with her back to the window, her hands clasped demurely in front of her.

"I suppose I could wait forever for you to ask me to come with you."

"Karen," Fargo said, "you're asking for feelings I don't have. I'm concerned for your safety. Isn't that enough?"

She sighed and said, "I suppose it will have to be. So what do we do now?"

"Well, you stay in this room until I come to get you, and then we'll have something to eat."

"And what are you going to do in the meantime?" she asked.

"I still have to ask Johnny Lang some questions."

"So you're going to face him and his cousins?"

"I don't think his cousins will be a problem," Fargo said. "I just have to convince Johnny that it's smarter to talk to me than go up against me. His cousins will go along with whatever he decides."

"I hope you're right," she said. "If you get yourself killed, I will be stuck in this town—and I know what I'll end up doing to survive."

"There's a lot more you could do, Karen."

"But there's not a lot more I'm experienced at," she said, "so just make sure you don't get killed. Okay?"

"Okay," he said. "I'll see you in a little while."

After he left, she stood at the window until he appeared on the street. She watched him until he disappeared from view, fervently hoping he'd be back.

Fargo looked around town for the Langs, but didn't find them. He went back to the saloon, where he'd had his first altercation with the cousins, and talked to the same bartender.

"Sure, I know where to find them," the barman said, "but why would you want to?"

"I got to ask one of them a question."

"Which one?"

"Johnny."

"I heard what happened," the man said. "He was in here a little while ago, looking for his cousins himself. He wasn't very happy."

"I know that."

"And you still want to find them?"

"It's not a question of what I want," Fargo said, "it's a question of what I have to do."

"Well, they live in a shack north of town. If you take the main road out . . ."

Fargo memorized the man's directions, then thanked him and left.

It was almost dark by the time he found the shack the Langs called home. He left his horse in a stand of trees far enough away that he wouldn't be heard and approached the shack on foot. He moved to a window and looked inside. It was a rundown one-room shack with four pallets spread around for beds. A table with four chairs sat near a stove. At the moment all four Langs were seated at the table, and Johnny was doing all the talking. It wasn't hard to imagine what he was talking about.

Fargo decided to be direct in his approach. He walked to the front door, drew his gun, and kicked the door open.

Three of them sat stunned, but Johnny Lang stood up and went for his gun, just the one he needed alive to talk.

"Don't!" he shouted, but Johnny was beyond hearing. As he drew his gun from his holster, Fargo shot him in the most non-lethal place he could think of, the thigh. Johnny yelped and went down. He dropped his gun and grabbed his right thigh.

"Bastard!" he said through gritted teeth. "Get him!"

"Who's next?" Fargo asked, covering them all with his gun.

"Take it easy," one of the brothers said.

"Take your guns out with your fingertips and toss them across the room. Do it!"

They did, all three guns clattering across the floor to the other side of the room.

"Now, down on your bellies, hands behind your necks. Don't make me tell you again!"

They did as they were told.

"You gonna shoot us in the back?" Danny Lang asked.

"I'm not going to shoot you at all if you don't make me," Fargo said. "Just lie still while I talk to your cousin."

"I need a doctor," Johnny said between clenched teeth.

"Well," Fargo said, crouching down, but not too close, "if you answer my questions, maybe I'll let your cousins get you to one."

"I'm not telling you shit!"

"Then we'll just wait here while you bleed to death."

Johnny Lang was trying desperately to stanch the flow of blood from his thigh, but he didn't know how.

"I'll bleed to death before I can tell you what you want to know."

Fargo moved closer and made sure Johnny had a clear view of the gun.

"Here, put your hands here"—he pointed—"and squeeze right there. See? Not bleeding so bad now."

He backed away before Johnny could get any ideas.

"Now, ready to talk?"

"Whataya wanna know?"

"Who told you about me? Who told you to hurt me, or kill me—"

"Just to slow you down."

"Who?"

"His name is Sam Kyle."

Fargo didn't know the name.

"What's he look like?"

Johnny gave him a description that could have fit dozens of men.

"Go on," Fargo said, "tell me what happened. If you make me ask, you will bleed to death before we're through."

"He rode into town and came to see me," Johnny said, speaking very quickly. "I think he wanted the sheriff, but he made do with me. He didn't know you were on his trail. He just paid me to slow down anybody who came through town looking for strangers."

"That's it?"

"That's all!" Johnny said frantically.

"Was he alone?"

"Yes."

"Did you know him before this?"

"No."

"Do you know where he was going from here?"

"No."

"And he left town that same day?"

"Yes."

"When?"

"I don't know . . . a couple of days ago."

"How much did he pay you?"

Johnny stopped then, his eyes flickering over to where his cousins were lying on the floor. Apparently, he'd been paid more than he told them, and he didn't want to give that away, not even in his present condition.

"A lot," he finally said.

"I'll accept that." Fargo stood up. "I'm going to

spend the night in town and leave in the morning," he said. "If I see any of you between now and when I leave, I'll kill you. Got that?"

"Yeah," Johnny said.

"You three?"

They all answered.

"Don't listen to Johnny, boys," Fargo advised. "As soon as his leg is patched up, he's going to want revenge on me. He's going to end up getting you all killed."

Johnny fixed Fargo with a murderous look.

"This ain't over."

"Then maybe I should kill you right now," Fargo said, pointing his gun at Johnny's head.

"Yeah," Johnny Lang said, "maybe you better."

Fargo thought about it, then rejected the idea. He'd have to do a lot of explaining to the sheriff. As it was, he was probably going to have to do some.

"You boys remember what I said," he told the three prone men. "When I leave, you can get your cousin to town for a doctor."

He looked at Johnny Lang.

"Be smart, Johnny."

Johnny spat, and it fell short several feet of landing on Fargo's boot.

"Or not," Fargo said, then left.

He rode back to town, left his horse at the livery, and walked to the hotel.

"Mr. Fargo?" the clerk called as he walked to the stairs.

"Yes?"

"The telegraph operator left this for you."

Fargo walked to the desk and accepted the piece of paper from the clerk. He hadn't expected an answer, but it didn't totally surprise him that one had come.

"Thanks. How much longer will the dining room be open?" he asked.

"An hour or so. I'll make sure you have plenty of time."

"Thanks."

He didn't read the telegram in the lobby, but waited until he was in the upstairs hall. When he finished it, he went down the hall to the room where Karen was waiting and knocked on the door.

They were the last ones in the dining room, which suited Fargo fine. He wasn't sure if his warning would be enough to keep the cousins from following Johnny Lang's lead. Killing them would have been more certain, but messy.

"Are you going to tell me about the telegram?" she asked.

He handed it to her so she could read it herself.

"I knew it," she said, handing it back.

"Dave's backing me, and Hodge is trying to get me on a wanted poster," he said, tucking the telegram into his pocket.

"And what happened with the Langs?"

While they ate—beef stew, which was all that was left in the kitchen, and suited them—he told her what had occurred.

"You stopped all four of them?" she asked, impressed. "And only had to shoot one?"

"I got lucky," he said.

"Do you think they'll stay away tonight?"

"I don't know," he said. "I hope so."

"Maybe we should leave now."

"Sneaking out at night isn't the answer," he said. "We'll just take precautions."

"What kind?"

"I'll show you when we get back to the room."

"You're not going to stay awake all night, are you?"

"No."

"Because I can take a turn watching."

"I'm sure you can, Karen, but it won't be necessary. Let's just finish eating and get up to the room. If we turn in early, we can get an early start."

"An early start to where?" she asked. "We don't know where the man is going."

"We know his name now," Fargo said, "and I'll just have to continue to track him."

"Sure," she said, "if he keeps that horse."

"You don't get rid of a good horse."

"What if it gets injured?"

"We'll just have to hope it doesn't," Fargo said.

"Okay, okay," she said, "you win. We'll just keep tracking him."

She sounded exasperated, but Fargo knew that deep down Karen was very happy to be going along.

14

They awoke the next morning after an uneventful night. When they had gone back to the room, Fargo showed Karen the precautions they were going to take. It involved using the pitcher and basin from the dresser top as alarms, one propped against the window and the other against the door. No one would be able to enter without knocking one down, which would wake them up. Fargo had his gun belt hanging on the bedpost all night.

At first Karen couldn't sleep because she was listening for the booby traps, but she finally woke the next morning, surprised that she had fallen asleep.

"If we don't stop to have breakfast," Fargo told her, "we can get out of here sooner and avoid more trouble."

"That suits me."

"We can stop along the way and have something to eat."

They checked out of the hotel and went to the livery to saddle their horses. While they were doing so, Fargo heard the scrape of a boot above his head, and saw some hay floating down from between the floorboards.

"Down!" he shouted to Karen. He pushed her to the

floor with one hand and drew his gun with the other. Suddenly, there was a shot, and a bullet plowed through the boards above his head. Fargo didn't hesitate. He pumped four shots very quickly through the boards into what he assumed was the hayloft. He heard a grunt, some footsteps, and then somebody fell out of the hayloft to the dirt floor of the livery.

Karen started to get up, but Fargo said, "Stay down."

He walked to the body to make sure the man was dead.

"You can come out now," he said finally. "He's dead."

"Who is it?" she asked.

As she came out of the stall, he rolled the body onto its back, and she saw the face of Johnny Lang—only she had never seen him before.

"It's the deputy," Fargo said, then added, "the ex-deputy."

"What about his cousins?"

Fargo looked up and listened a moment.

"They don't seem to be around," he said.

"I guess this one is the only one you didn't make an impression on."

"Well," Fargo said, ejecting spent shells from his gun, "I guess I made one now."

As a result of the shooting, they weren't able to leave as easily as they wanted to. Fargo and Karen explained to the sheriff what had happened, and the man accepted their version.

"It's not like he's got another story," he said, looking down at Lang. "Reckon you can finish saddling up and head out."

"Thanks, Sheriff."

"I'd appreciate not seeing you back here, though," the lawman added.

"Oh," Fargo said, "I think that can be arranged."

They rode until noon, then stopped to eat some beef jerky and rest the horses. Fargo had picked up the trail again just outside of town, and they were following it.

"Do you think the cousins will come after us?" she asked.

"I doubt it," Fargo said. "Johnny was the brains. Without the brain, the body dies."

"So what do we do now?"

"Keep tracking."

"I can't help thinking we're tracking a horse, not knowing who's riding it."

"You can't help thinking it because that's exactly what we're doing—at least, we were."

"What do you mean?"

"We tracked it that way until we reached Carmody. Now, thanks to Johnny Lang, we know the man's name."

"Sam Kyle," she said.

"Right."

"Do you know that name?"

"I never heard it before."

"So then he's not, uh, famous, like you?"

"If you mean he doesn't have a reputation, apparently you're right. Maybe he's in the process of building one for himself."

"Do we know what he looks like?"

"According to Johnny, he's sort of average height, average weight, brown hair . . . could be anybody."

"Nothing distinctive, so we can recognize him when we see him?"

"No."

"Do you think Johnny was telling you the truth?"

"I think so," Fargo said. "He was bleeding, and he wanted medical attention. I don't believe he thought to lie. Of course, he was probably angry about that later."

"Which is why he crawled up into the hayloft to wait for you."

"Right."

"That was too close for comfort," she said. "It's a good thing your instincts are so great."

"They've kept me alive this long." He popped a last bit of jerky into his mouth, and she did the same.

"Ready?" he asked.

"Sure."

They mounted up and started riding again, Fargo keeping his head down, his eyes on the ground. As hard as Karen tried, she just couldn't see the things he saw.

"Skye?"

"Yep?"

"How do you think Hodge is doing? I mean, about getting a wanted poster out on you?"

"I think Dave will be able to hold him off, at least for a while."

"And then what?"

"Well, by then I hope to have the money back."

"You're an optimist."

113

"It's better than thinking negatively," Fargo said. "I can't even think about Kyle and his boys getting away with the money."

"That's your male ego talking."

"You're probably right."

"You don't want to admit that someone got the better of you."

"Right again."

"So you're going to prove you're better by finding them and getting the money back."

"That's the general idea."

She shook her head.

"It must be very hard to be a man."

"And it's not hard to be a woman?"

"We're not always puffing our chests out and beating them," she said.

He glanced at her chest.

"You women look pretty well puffed out to me."

"See?" she said. "Now you're showing your animal instincts. They always come out in sex and in fighting."

"I'm not having sex," he said, "and I'm not fighting."

"You've been fighting somebody all your life, haven't you?"

"Is this going to turn into a serious discussion about men and women?" he asked. "Are you going to tell me you haven't been fighting all your life?"

"It's different."

"Why?"

"Because women fight for survival."

"And why do men fight?"

"It's an instinct," she said, "and they like it. They—you—can't help yourself. Somebody slights you, or bests you, and you have to fight with them."

"Nobody's bested me."

"See?" she said. "You can't even admit it."

"Oh no," he said, "I'm not going to let you reduce me to someone who fights only from instinct while you—women—are so noble that you only fight to survive."

"Prove me wrong."

"How?"

"Turn around," she said. "Let's go back to Fort Leavenworth, tell them the money was stolen, tell them what we know, and let them hire detectives to find the money."

"That's just silly."

"Why?"

"Because we're on the trail," he said. "If we waited that long, the trail would grow cold."

"You know something I just realized?"

"What?"

"You're right."

"I am?"

"Sure," she said. "If we go back and they hire somebody to track down this money, it would probably just be you."

He thought a moment, then said, "You're probably right."

And that ended the discussion about men and women.

"Well, this looks different," Fargo said.

115

"What does?"

He stood up and stared ahead. They had just passed a town limit sign that said: NEW BERRY. Two words, not one. No population figure.

"This is the main road into town."

"So?"

"He's staying on it."

"So?"

"He also met up with someone else here," Fargo said. "There's two sets of tracks here now."

"One of the other robbers?"

"Maybe, but whoever it was came *from* the town to meet him."

"Or maybe," she said, "he's double-crossing them and meeting someone here to split the money with."

"That could be, too."

"Or maybe it's the person he was supposed to meet," she suggested.

"We could play this game all day," Fargo said. "We've been on the trail now for almost five days since we left Carmody. I'm ready for some hot food again."

"And another bath."

"Maybe one with less of an audience this time?" he asked.

"Definitely."

Fargo mounted up, then looked at Karen.

"Okay," he said. "Maybe it will all end in the town of New Berry."

"That would be nice," she said. "I don't know who's more tired, me or my horse."

15

New Berry fell somewhere between Carmody and Barlow in size. However, it seemed to be teeming with people, which certainly set it apart from the almost ghost town atmosphere of Barlow. Carmody was surely a bigger town, but New Berry felt like it had more people.

"What's going on?" Karen wondered as they tried to negotiate the main street and avoid the people who were crossing the street, or congregating in it. "Can it be like this every day?"

"Must be some sort of holiday," Fargo said, and at that moment they came to a bend in the street. They saw a banner hanging above the street that said: FOUNDER'S DAY CELEBRATION, HAPPY 10TH!

"That explains it," he said. "It's the town's tenth birthday."

People were actually jostling their horses now because the street near the banner was crowded with them.

"Let's stop here," Fargo said. "We can find the livery later."

They halted in front of a hotel called the Newberry House and tied off their horses. A man staggered into

Karen and would have knocked her down if Fargo hadn't grabbed her.

"Oh, sorry, ma'am," he said, turning and doffing his hat. He was young, and skinny, and also drunk. "Say, you're a pretty one."

"Thanks," Karen said, and the man disappeared into the crowd.

"This is great," Fargo said. "How are we going to spot our man in this crowd when every other man we see fits his description?"

Karen shook her head as they entered the hotel.

"Sorry," the clerk said when they approached the desk, "no rooms. Founder's Day, you know?"

"No, we didn't know," Fargo said, leaning on the desk. "Is there anyplace in town we could get a room?"

"Nope," the clerk said.

"How do you know?"

"Because people have been coming into town all week," the man said. "Even the townspeople who had rooms to rent are full up. There's not a room in town to be had."

"And it's been like that all week?"

"All week."

Fargo looked at Karen, who said, "How about food?"

"Is your dining room open?" Fargo asked.

"Sure is, and there's plenty of room, because everybody's out on the street."

"At least we can sit down and have a meal and get away from the crowds," Fargo said to Karen, and led her into the room.

They had the dining room to themselves, and they

took their time. They finished lunch off with coffee and peach pie.

"So what are we going to do now?" Karen asked. "If we've got nowhere to stay, maybe he has the same problem—if he's even here."

"The way I figure it," Fargo said, "whoever met him came from town, so they probably had a room, or rooms, already."

"Great," Karen said, "so he's got a place to stay."

"We'll find something," Fargo said. "Maybe a hayloft in the livery."

"That sounds comfortable."

"Actually, that wouldn't be bad," Fargo said. "It would give me a chance to check out all the horses there."

"Oh, right," she said, "still looking for that distinctive hoofprint."

"At least then we'd know he was here."

Karen put her fork down and stared across the table at Fargo. "Skye, this seems hopeless," she said. "I mean, we don't even know what this guy looks like, and this town is overflowing with people. He could have been the man who bumped into me out front, for all we know."

"Nobody said this would be easy, Karen."

"Your optimism infuriates me sometimes."

"It's the only way I can function," Fargo said. "I know it's going to be hard to find our man in a town overflowing with people, but I can't let that stop me from trying."

"So you find his horse," she said. "Then what? How do you find him?"

"I don't."

"What?"

"I watch the horse."

She stared at him, then sat back in her chair, letting her arms dangle at her sides.

"What's wrong?"

"That's so simple."

"Yes, it is."

"You let me sit here ranting, and all the while you knew how you were going to find him—and it's so simple. I feel so *stupid*."

"Well," Fargo said, "in order for it to work, I still have to find his horse."

"I guess you really do know what you're doing."

"You're just discovering that now?" he asked.

Fargo and Karen worked their way through the street, pushed and jostled along the way, until they reached the livery.

"Sounds like one helluva good time out there," the liveryman said by way of greeting.

"Why aren't you there?" Karen asked.

The man was in his sixties and had an arm that had been broken at least once and not set right, so that it stuck out at an odd angle. He moved as if he had bad knees and sore hips, and he had the scarred hands of a man who had been around horses and their teeth his whole life.

"I don't party, missy," he said. "Not with these old bones. Somethin' I can do fer you?"

"We've got two horses, but we can't get them

120

through the crowd," Fargo said. "Do you have any stall space?"

"I got one," the man said. "If you can fit both of your horses in there together, it's yours."

"That's fine," Fargo said.

"Still gotta pay for two."

"That's fine also," Fargo said, "but now tell me if you have any space in your hayloft."

The man cackled and said, "Can't get a hotel room, huh?"

"Nope."

"Well," the man said, scratching his stubble, "guess I could let you sleep up there, but you'd have to pay for another stall."

"Sounds reasonable," Fargo said. "We're much obliged."

Fargo paid the man in advance, and then he and Karen took their horses into the livery.

"Is this going to be just like Carmody?" she asked. "I take care of the horses and you look at the other horses' hooves?"

"No," he said, "I'll take care of the horses."

"You want me to look at the other ones?"

"You're going to have to help me because there are a lot of them," he said as they reached the one empty stall. "Hope these animals get along in here," he said.

"I hope we get along in the hayloft," she said.

He smiled and said, "Oh, I think we will."

She smiled back.

"But first we're going to have to do some work," he said. "Take care of our animals, then start looking at all the other ones."

"You're going to have to tell me specifically what to look for," she said.

He did so while they were unsaddling and caring for their horses. The two animals seemed undisturbed that they had to share a stall and a feed bin. They just dug in and began to chow down.

"Well," Fargo said, "so far, so good."

"When do we start looking?" she asked.

"Tonight, when everybody is asleep and we come back here to sleep. No one will be around, and we can look at the other horses freely without being caught."

"So what if we're caught?" she asked. "We're just looking at their damn feet."

"Tell that to some cowboy who comes in and finds you messing with his horse. The first thing he's going to think is that you're trying to steal it—and that could get you shot. No, we'll wait until no one's around, and we have all the time in the world."

"So what do we do in the meantime?" she asked. "Join the revelers?"

"I don't particularly feel like celebrating the birth of this town," he said. "What I'd like to do is get a drink and relax for a while, and then maybe come back here and get some sleep even before we start inspecting the other horses."

"That sounds good to me, too."

They walked through the stable to the front doors. When they stepped outside, they could hear lots of noise from town, including music.

"You know," she said, "it might take some time for this town to go to sleep tonight."

122

"I know it," Fargo said. "I wonder if we'll be able to get a quiet drink somewhere."

"What are the chances of finding a quiet saloon in this town tonight?" she asked.

He didn't answer.

16

While they were in the saloon, something occurred to Fargo that he didn't like. Even with the place as packed as it was—with men *and* women—what if their man, Sam Kyle, was there and he recognized one of them? Fargo had to calculate whether or not that was possible. When Kyle had seen him, he was very likely flying through the air. Could Kyle have seen Karen well enough to recognize her when she was pinned beneath the judge's dead body?

Of course, the other possibility was that Zack Wheeler told Kyle that the Trailsman was riding shotgun on the stage. Possibly Kyle might remember him from that. On the other hand, if Kyle had known who he was, wouldn't he have made sure he was dead at the scene of the robbery? That would have been the smart thing to do.

So, there was a possibility of being recognized, but there *were* a lot of people in town for Founder's Day, and there *were* a heck of a lot of people in the saloon at that moment.

"What are you thinking?" Karen asked. She had to shout to be heard over the din.

Rather than answer, Fargo shook his head at her. He

didn't want to shout their conversation. He'd tell her later.

"Well," she said when they were outside and walking back to the livery, "he couldn't recognize me. You didn't even see me under the judge until I moaned."

"So if he recognized anyone, it would be me," Fargo said.

"Isn't it a little late to be worrying about that?" she asked. "We're here, and we're committed."

"You're right about that,"

When they got to the livery, a side door had been left open for them. They had been instructed, though, to lock it when they entered, which they did.

Inside, Fargo lit a lamp and hung it from a post. It illuminated the entire interior.

"We've got the whole place to ourselves," he said, "and can't be disturbed."

"Oh, my," she said, "what should we do first?"

He looked at her.

"I know," she said. "Check horses' hooves."

"You can go to sleep in the hayloft if you want," he offered. "I can do this."

"I want to help," she said. "Besides, the quicker you finish, the quicker I get you in the hayloft with me."

"That's an incentive no man could resist," he said, smiling.

Fargo started at one end and Karen at the other. Before doing so, Fargo made sure she knew what she was looking for, and that he wouldn't have to double-check her. They were about halfway through the stable when Karen called out excitedly, "I think I found it!"

Fargo went over to the stall she was standing in. She was holding up the horse's right hind leg, and he saw the little cutout in the soft part of its hoof. He leaned over and cleaned the hoof out with his hand so he could get a better look.

"That's it," he said. "You found it."

"He's here then."

"His horse is here," Fargo said. "Most likely he's here, too."

She was very excited. "What do we do now?"

"Now we get some sleep," he said.

"And tomorrow?"

"We'll have to watch the horse and see if he shows up here."

"But he'd only come to get the horse if he was leaving town," she said. "What if he's not leaving tomorrow?"

"Then we'll have to watch for him the day after that, and the day after that, until he—or someone—does show up for the horse."

"You think he might send someone else for it?"

"It's possible."

"And then we'd have to follow that person to get to him."

"Right."

"When you're hunting a man, is it always this exciting when you get so close to catching him?"

"I don't know," he said. "I'm not a bounty hunter, Karen. I don't hunt men for a living."

"I'm sorry," she said, "I just meant . . . I don't know what I meant, really."

"It's all right," he said. "Let's just go up into the hayloft and get some sleep."

Fargo got their blankets and the lamp and climbed up the ladder after Karen. She had only been up there a few moments before him, but when he got there she was naked.

The light from the lamp made her pale skin seem yellow, and her brown nipples were an odd shade in that light. Her breasts cast shadows on her ribs, and the tangle of hair between her legs was a shadowing mystery. He could smell her skin, and her readiness. He guessed that being this close to getting her man had really excited her. He couldn't object to that.

"Come on," she said, "spread out the blankets. I don't want to get hay in my . . . well, you know where."

Fargo spread the blankets, then removed his gun belt and, slowly, his own clothes. Her scent grew sharper as he undressed, and by the time he was naked, he was long and hard.

"God," she said, grabbing him and pulling him down on the blankets with her.

He got between her legs, grabbed her ankles, and pulled her legs apart. He drove himself into her wet core, plunging hard and deep. He kept her legs up so that he could kiss her feet and ankles, then stroke her thighs as he poked in and out of her slowly.

"Ooooh, yes, yessss," she groaned, "harder, come on, harder . . . split me apart!"

He didn't take her literally, but he knew she wanted it harder, so he gave it to her. He released her legs so that they dropped down to the blankets, braced himself

127

on either side of her with his arms so that he was hovering right over her, taking her in long, hard strokes.

"Oh, Skye, yes, that's it," she said, "that's it . . . ohhh . . ."

Abruptly, when he felt he was wet enough, he withdrew from her and roughly turned her over.

She got up on her hands and knees and presented her backside to him. This was a position not many men wanted—not the men who had come to her as customers. Most of them simply want to slam it into her until they came, and then go downstairs for some more whiskey.

"God, you feel so good," she said, "so big! It feels like you're here." She touched her fingers to a place between her breasts.

Slowly, he began to move again, in and out, never totally out, but in and out nevertheless. She began to move with him, finding his rhythm, and then matching it. He reached around to pinch her nipples at the same time. When they had the same tempo, he pulled her up so that she was on her knees and he was able to use his hands all over her. He slid one hand between her legs. When he found her stiff little nub, he began to circle it with one finger.

"Oh, Goddddd!" she moaned. "Jesus, I never . . . no one's ever . . . mmmm." She pressed her lips together as he released her so she could go back down on all fours. In this position he grasped her hips and began to move in and out of her harder still. He grunted with the effort of taking her, and the air was filled with the scent of their sex and their sweat.

She experienced several spasms of pleasure, while Fargo continued to hold back.

He leaned over her at this point and said, "Move with me. Lie on your side."

They lay down together without losing the penetration. Now they were spooned, and she was lying on one of his arms. With that hand he found one breast and began to knead it, pinching the nipple, while the other hand he reached down between her legs to touch her there again. All the while he was moving in and out of her.

"Oooooh," she moaned, burying her face in his arm, and the trio of sensations began to push her over the edge. "Yes, yes, yes," she groaned. "Oh, God, you're killing me, Skye . . . it's wonderful!"

Their bodies grew slick with perspiration, and suddenly she stiffened, catching her breath, and then started to buck against him. The movement was such that she tightened around him, and that was all it took. Suddenly, he erupted inside her and began to empty himself into her. It seemed to go on and on for a long time, as she milked more from him than he thought he had to give . . . and more and still more until it was almost painful.

17

Fargo had to move because Karen had fallen asleep on his gun arm. Even though they were locked in the livery together, with no one else around, he couldn't be comfortable with that arm pinned down. He tried to slide carefully from beneath her, but she woke up anyway.

"I'm sorry," he said in a soothing voice. "I was trying not to wake you. Go back to sleep."

"What's wrong?"

"Nothing," he said. "I just want to check on the horses."

He climbed down the ladder from the hayloft, still naked, carrying the lamp. Karen moved to the edge of the loft so she could watch him. He moved so confidently, even while totally naked. He went into the stall where their two horses were and spoke to both animals in a soothing tone—almost the same tone he had used on her when telling her to go back to sleep.

"Are they all right?" she called out.

"They're fine," he said. "They were just bumping into each other some."

He left the stall and climbed back into the hayloft,

turning the flame on the lamp down low before setting it aside.

"You know," she said, "if we had kicked that over before, we could have burned this stable down."

He lay down next to her and said, "I don't think either one of us would have noticed."

"I wouldn't have," she said. She lay down on his arm—the left one—and snuggled close to him. "I never had a man do that to me before."

"What, you mean—"

"No," she said. "I've had men do *that* to me before, but never like you did, never with such . . . *concern* for my pleasure. You're a rare man, Skye Fargo."

"I like to think so."

"The woman who ends up with you is going to be very lucky."

He didn't respond.

"I wasn't—"

"I know," he said. "Go back to sleep."

She snuggled close, but didn't fall asleep right away. He could tell by her breathing. He wondered what she was thinking. They had spent a lot of time together, been through a lot together. He wondered how she would take it when they had to split up for good. If it hadn't been for their difficulties, it would have happened in Carmody. It might have been easier then. Instead, all these extra days, and extra emotions, and extra . . . incidents had been added on to their relationship.

Finally, when she did fall asleep, he stopped wondering what she was thinking and started wondering what she was dreaming about.

                              *   *   *

They awoke in the morning and found it was more
difficult to dress in the confines of the hayloft than it
had been to get undressed. They had come down the
ladder and extinguished the lamp just as the big front
doors opened and the liveryman came in.

"Sleep well?" he asked.

"Very well," Karen said.

He looked at them both, then smiled knowingly.
That was when Karen realized how disheveled she
must look.

"Is there anyplace in town a lady could get a bath?"
she asked.

"You could try the barber shop," he said. "They
don't get many women in there, but then these last few
days ain't been normal ones, with all these people in
town and all."

"I'll give it a try," she said.

She walked outside with Fargo. "What are you
going to do?" she asked.

"I have to stay here in case he shows up," he said.
"You go and have your bath. If the barber shop won't
let you, try the hotel."

"I'll be back as soon as I can," she said. "I could
watch for a while while you get a bath . . . or something."

"Have something to eat, too," he said. "We'll have
to do everything in shifts until we resolve this."

"All right," she said. "I'll be back as soon as I can."

She seemed about to kiss him, then thought better of
it and simply touched his arm before leaving.

Fargo went back inside to talk to the liveryman.

"I got a lot of horses in here," the man said, rubbing his jaw. "Don't rightly know I can put a man's face to 'em, right off."

"You know my horse, don't you?"

"Sure," the man said. "You got the one's sharing a stall with another one. See? That's easy."

"This was recent," Fargo said, "maybe a day or two before we got here." He described Sam Kyle to the man, who frowned and scratched his jaw.

"Sounds like a lot of fellas I seen this week," he said. "Sorry."

"That's okay," Fargo said.

"Fella owe you money?"

"Something like that," Fargo said, and walked away.

A couple of hours passed before Karen returned, smelling fresh and clean and seeming much happier. She joined Fargo in the hayloft.

"I just soaked in the tub and thought about what we did up here last night," she said dreamily.

"Really? And how did that make you feel?"

"Like I wanted to do it again."

"Well," he said, "maybe that can be arranged."

"I can watch the horses for a while," she said. "Why don't you go and . . . do what you want to do?"

"I guess I'll just do what we've been doing from town to town," he said. "Talk to the local sheriff."

"Some of them aren't very cooperative, are they?" she asked.

"Most of them don't want any trouble in their town," Fargo said, "and will do what they can to avoid it."

"I suppose you've known a lot of them over the years," she said. "Lawmen, I mean."

"Oh yeah," he said, "good ones, not so good ones . . . really bad ones."

"Well, I hope this town has a good one."

"I'll find out," he said, "and I'll send another telegram to Dave Silver in Fort Leavenworth and give him an update."

"You'll be telling Hodge where you are."

"I realize that," he said, "but if he tries to send someone after us, it'll all be over by the time they get here."

"I hope you're right."

"Listen to me very carefully," he said. "If anyone comes for that horse, get a good look, but don't do anything else."

"But that's silly—"

"Karen."

"—I'd have to follow them to see where they—"

"Karen! Just do as I tell you. This is not a game. Kyle is a dangerous man."

"All right," she said. "Okay, I'll get a good look."

"Good."

"But what if he mounts up and rides out?" she asked. "What then?"

"We won't be far behind," Fargo said. "In fact, that might even be best. It might be easier to handle him on the trail than in a town as full of people as this one."

"Innocent bystanders, huh?"

"And that wouldn't make the local sheriff very happy at all," he said, and left.

*　　*　　*

"This doesn't make me very happy at all, Fargo," the local sheriff said.

"Can't say as I blame you, Sheriff," Fargo said. "You've got a lot of people in town."

"We're busting at the seams," Sheriff Marc Ryan said. "I hate these damn Founder's Day celebrations. Founder's *Day*." He almost spat. "The damn thing goes on for days."

Ryan was in his mid-thirties and had been sheriff of New Berry for three years, following a four-year stint as deputy. He was tall, with narrow shoulders and big hands. He was an odd-looking man who appeared as if he'd been put together from parts of different men, but he also exuded an air of competence that Fargo liked.

He leaned back in his chair now and stared at the ceiling. "I always imagine the worst when this time of the year comes," he said. "The town's busting, the liquor's flowing, and you know what?"

"What?"

He looked at Fargo. "Nothing ever really goes wrong. Seven years I've been here, and in seven years there's been no serious trouble. I'd like to keep it that way."

"Again, I don't blame you," Fargo said. "If I can take this out of town, I will, Sheriff."

"You've got no official standing in this, right, Fargo?"

"That's right."

"You were riding shotgun, and you've taken it upon yourself to track these men down."

"Right again."

"Are you going to be looking for a reward? Is that it?" the man asked.

"Are you asking me if I'm a bounty hunter, Sheriff?"

"I'm just trying to get a handle on you, Fargo," he said. "I know your reputation, and I've never heard that you hunted for bounty."

"And I'm not now," Fargo said. "I'm trying to get back the money I was supposed to be guarding. It was my responsibility."

"Okay," Ryan said, nodding. "I can understand that. So what are your plans?"

"We're going to watch his horse until he—or someone—shows up for it."

"We?"

"I'm here with a woman," Fargo said, and explained who Karen was and what her part was.

"You know, I think I heard something about this holdup," Ryan said. "Wasn't there a judge in the coach?"

"That's right. Judge William P. Server."

"Seems I heard there's a posse out, a federal posse."

Fargo waited. Had the word been spread that they were looking for him?

"I haven't seen any paper on you, Fargo."

"That's good."

"But if I get word that the posse is looking for you—"

"You'll do your job, Sheriff," Fargo said. "I understand that."

Ryan sighed and rubbed his hand over his face, then stood up.

"I've got to go on my rounds. I'm sorry I can't help you as far as strangers in town, but you understand there are a lot of them."

"I do understand, but from the tracks I saw it appeared to me that someone from town rode out to meet him."

"So you're suggesting that maybe he's staying with someone who lives here?"

"Or someone who got here early enough to get a room."

"But not in Sam Kyle's name."

"Right."

The sheriff frowned as he put on his hat. "I don't seem to know that name. I don't recall seeing any paper on him, but I'll look through the posters I've got when I get back."

"That would be helpful."

"And you'll be at the livery?"

"Yes."

They walked to the door together and went outside.

"I'll let you know if I find anything," Ryan said, pulling the office door closed behind him.

"Much obliged, Sheriff," Fargo said, and the two men went their separate ways.

Fargo didn't think Sheriff Marc Ryan could be bought, not like the deputy in Carmody. This man seemed to take his job very seriously, but now someone knew that he and Karen were at the livery, so just to play it safe he was going to be extra alert.

18

Fargo went from the sheriff's office to the telegraph office. It was getting on toward afternoon, and once again the carnival atmosphere was starting to take over the town.

He entered the telegraph office and wrote out his message to Dave Silver. "I'll wait for a reply," he said, sure that Dave would reply promptly. He'd be very anxious to know about his money.

Fargo waited half an hour before the reply came in. He thanked the clerk and took it outside to read.

Fargo,
    Recover funds as fast as you can. Hodge convinced a federal marshal to start looking for you.
Dave

Fargo folded up the telegram and tucked it into his shirt pocket. If a federal marshal was on his trail, he thought, word would get around. If Sam Kyle was in town, he had to find him and locate that money. What would the man do with the money once he got here? Would he have the nerve to deposit it in a bank? Or would he just hide it somewhere? If he did hat, how could Fargo hope to locate it? No, as much as he wanted to become more active, they simply had to wait and watch the horse and hope he was right, that the horse was Sam Kyle's, and that he'd come for it.

Fargo left the telegraph office and went back to the livery stable.

He told Karen about the telegram and let her read it.

"He's warning you."

"Yes."

"And he won't show this to Hodge?"

"I don't think so."

"I hope not," she said, handing it back to him.

"Anyone come near the horse?"

"No one."

"Anyone come in at all?"

"No," she said. "I get the feeling that anyone who's gonna be in town is here already."

"I agree."

"How was the sheriff?"

He relayed his conversation to her and told her that he approved of the man. "He seems to know his job, and he wasn't overly suspicious of me."

"He knew your reputation?"

"Yes."

"Maybe that was why."

"Whatever the reason, he listened to me. That's all I was asking him to do."

"He doesn't know anything about strangers in town?" she asked.

Fargo shook his head. "There are too damn many here."

"I can believe that."

They sat together for a few minutes, watching the horse, and then she said, "I'm hungry."

"So am I."

"What do we do? Eat in shifts?"

"I guess so."

"Why don't I go and get something and bring it back?" she suggested. "We can have a picnic up here."

"A picnic?"

"Why not?"

He looked at her, then said, "Why not?"

She got to her feet. "I'll find a cafe and have them put together a basket for us."

"Good idea," he said. "I'll wait here."

She laughed and said, "Where else would you go? I'll be back as soon as I can."

He watched her go down the ladder and for a moment wondered if he should be letting her go. He pushed the thought away and fastened his eyes on the horse.

An hour later, he knew he shouldn't have let her go. Two hours later, he knew that the game had changed. The only reason she'd be gone this long was if something had gone wrong, and the only way something could have gone wrong was if somebody had tipped off Sam Kyle.

He climbed down and asked the liveryman to ask Karen to wait there for him if she returned.

"Sure thing."

He went to see the sheriff again.

When he got to the sheriff's office, it was empty. He didn't know if the man had any deputies or not. He certainly should have, especially at a time like this when the town was so full of people.

He walked around town, looking for the sheriff. He'd gone on his rounds over two hours ago. Could he still be on them? Or was he with Sam Kyle, holding Karen somewhere?

Fargo couldn't believe he'd been wrong about Sheriff Ryan. He thought maybe there was another explanation for Karen's disappearance. Maybe she'd done something foolish and gotten caught at it. Could she have recognized Sam Kyle and followed him? Maybe she wasn't actually in danger. Maybe she was watching Kyle, waiting for a chance to get back to Fargo.

He went back to the livery to see if she'd returned, but the liveryman hadn't seen her.

Fargo was about to leave when the man said, "I did see somebody, though."

"Oh? Who?"

"Fella who owned that horse."

"What?"

Fargo went into the stable and saw that the horse was gone. "When did he come in?"

"Just after you left," the man said, "like he was watching and waiting for you to leave."

"Was it the fella I described?"

"Nope," the liveryman said, "different fella altogether."

"What'd he look like?"

"Young fella, maybe twenty or so, tall and skinny. Said he'd been sent to fetch the horse."

"And you didn't know him?"

"Never saw him before."

"Where'd he take the horse?"

"Don't know," the liveryman said, "but he took him out the back."

"Thanks."

Fargo went out the back and checked the ground. Sure enough, the tracks were there, with the distinctive mark. They were fresh, and all he had to do was follow them.

It was that easy.

Several hours later, Fargo had followed the tracks to a small shack on the outskirts of town. He saw the horse tied off outside with several others. All in all there were four, the same number there had been at the robbery. Apparently, the other three men who were in on the job had found their way here, as well, by another route. If he was lucky, all four of them were inside, with all of the money. If he wasn't lucky, there were others in on the job, as well.

He made his way to one side of the shack, mainly because he didn't have much of a choice. He peered in a window and saw three men lounging about, two of them drinking coffee and one sitting at a table, playing solitaire. In one corner of the room he saw the two moneybags from the bank in Leavenworth. Whether or not the money was still in them was something he could only guess at.

Three men inside, four horses outside. There was one man unaccounted for.

His thoughts and worries for Karen's safety had been set aside now. All he was thinking about was recovering that money.

Two of the men looked to be in their thirties. The one playing solitaire was about twenty, no doubt the one who had gone to the livery for the horse.

It was time for him to earn the money Dave Silver had paid him for riding shotgun on the stage. He walked around to the front door with a sense of having gone through this before. How many times had he faced odds like this—three to one, four to one, sometimes more? How many times had he come out on top, and how many more times would he?

Fargo drew his gun, wondering if this would go the same way it had gone with the Lang boys back in Carmody? Or was it Barlow? No, it was Carmody. It seemed as if this had all dragged on long enough. Time to end it.

He kicked open the door and stepped into the room. He was surprised by the reaction of the three men as he covered them. They all simply turned their heads and looked at him. The kid even took the time to put a black seven on a red eight.

"Right on time," one of the men said.

"Guns on the floors, gents."

All three complied, with no resistance.

"Where's the fourth man?" Fargo asked.

"He's around," the younger man said.

Fargo risked a quick look behind him, as if he expected to find the man there. He closed the door so he wouldn't be surprised.

"Just take it easy," he said, moving across the room to the moneybags. He picked one up and found it was empty. He kicked the other one. It was also empty.

"Where's the money?"

"In a safe place," one of them said.

"And where's Kyle? Sam Kyle?"

"Sam's around," the young man said.

Why were they so calm? Fargo wondered. Were they expecting Kyle to come in and resolve everything himself? Kyle had told them to expect Fargo. That's why one of them had said, "Right on time."

Only where was Kyle? Wasn't this his cue to come into the play?—if he was going to.

"Hmm," Fargo said, "look at this situation. No money, no Sam Kyle, just you three and me. What does that tell you, boys?"

The three men exchanged glances, then looked at the door. Were they expecting Kyle?

"I think we've all been had, gents," Fargo said. "The trail I followed here was too easy. It was supposed to be a trap, wasn't it? Only where's the spring? Where's Sam Kyle when you need him?"

The question was on the faces of all three men as they looked at each other.

19

They stood that way for a while, the four of them, waiting.

"Guess he's not coming," Fargo said finally.

The other three said nothing.

"Looks like he set you up."

Silence.

"No money, and you take the fall."

The three of them started looking at their guns on the floor. If they all went for the weapons, it would be dicey. He had to decide which one to take first, but none of them was showing any leadership qualities. It probably didn't matter.

The three of them started to sweat. The young one was biting his lip, his eyes darting between Fargo and his gun. Fargo guessed that he would be the first one to move, the first one to lose his patience.

And he was right.

The kid dove from his chair to the floor, hands scrabbling for his gun. Fargo took three quick steps and kicked the boy in the side of the head.

The other two moved then, going for their guns. Fargo shot one, then heard glass break and a man's voice yell, "This is the law. Hold it!"

But the second man didn't hold it, and the law—in the person of Sheriff Marc Ryan—shot him.

From the open window the sheriff looked at Fargo and said, "You called it."

"You might as well come inside," Fargo said. "We'll have to wake this one up."

Earlier, it had taken Fargo the better part of an hour and a half to finally track the sheriff down, and when he did, he explained the situation to him.

"You thought I tipped him?" the man had asked.

"The thought crossed my mind."

"And now?"

"Now I don't think so."

"What changed your mind?"

Fargo had told him, then explained what he wanted to do, and Ryan had agreed.

The sheriff entered the shack and looked at Fargo. Both men ejected their spent shells and replaced them with live ones, then holstered their guns.

"He played us all," Fargo said, "especially these three."

"Now what?"

"Now we wake him up. Maybe he can give us some idea where Kyle is."

They hauled the boy up, put him back in his chair, and slapped his face until he woke up. When he did, he became tense and looked around.

"They're dead," Fargo said. "You're the last one."

It slowly dawned on the boy that he and the others had actually been set up.

"That sonofabitch!"

"Now you get it," Fargo said. "Where is he, son?"

"I don't know!" the boy said angrily. "He was supposed to be here. He was supposed to come up behind you."

"But he didn't," Fargo said. "Instead, he left you here with the empty moneybags so that, dead or alive, you would all take the blame."

"Sonofabitch," the boy said again.

"Where's the money?" Fargo asked.

"In the bank."

"Why would he do that?" Ryan asked. "Put the money in the bank?"

"Maybe because he expected there to be no problems," Fargo said.

"But if he set you up, he knew you were here," Ryan said. "Who tipped him off?"

"I've got a bad feeling about that one," Fargo said. "A bad feeling."

Since the kid didn't seem to have any idea where Sam Kyle was, Fargo had no choice but to try the bank. If Kyle was expecting he and the other three to shoot it out, maybe he was preparing to get out of town.

"Wait for me," Ryan said. "I just have to put this young fella in a cell."

"I can't wait, Sheriff," Fargo said. "I've tracked this Kyle a long way. I can't let him get away now, especially not after this."

"You don't have any authority—"

"I'll head for the bank," he said. "You put him in a cell like you said and follow me."

"Fargo—" Sheriff Ryan called, but Fargo was gone.

*　　*　　*

New Berry's Front Street was full of people, as it had been the day before when they first arrived. Fargo kicked himself for not asking the sheriff where the bank was, but on his way back to the center of town, he recalled having passed it on the way in.

It was rough getting to it, though. Front Street was like one big, long circus, with people playing games and drummers hawking their wares. Finally, Fargo saw the bank, but just as he did, the front door opened, and Karen came out with a man. The man was holding her arm with one hand and carrying a satchel with the other. It didn't take a genius to realize what was in the satchel.

Fargo started to push people out of his way as he tried to get to the bank. The man didn't see him, but Karen did, and she yelled. "Fargo!"

The man whipped his head around, saw Fargo, and started pulling her. He got her in front of him, then started pushing. They were having the same trouble Fargo was, though, trying to get by people who were in no hurry to move out of the way.

Fargo realized that Karen and the man he assumed was Sam Kyle were heading in the direction of the livery stable. He couldn't increase his speed because for every body he pushed out of the way another two took its place. He was just going to have to do his best to get clear. It was about a three-block section of Front Street that was jam-packed, and as soon as he got clear of them, he'd be able to move faster. Unfortunately, Karen and Kyle were ahead of him, so they'd get clear first.

Fargo wondered if the sheriff would ever get through in time.

Fargo saw Karen and Kyle break free of the crowd finally, and then they started running. Unless they already had saddled horses waiting at the livery, they'd have to stop to saddle two.

It felt like ages to Fargo until he broke free of the crowd. It seemed as if men and women alike were clutching at him, trying to force him to stay, but finally he got free and ran for the livery. He heard a shot as he approached, and when he came within sight of it, he saw the liveryman lying on the ground outside. He couldn't tell if the man was dead or alive, but it was a pretty safe bet that Kyle and Karen were inside.

Fargo ran to the door and stopped, drawing his gun and flattening his back against the side of the building.

"Sam Kyle!" he called. "It's all over, Kyle. The sheriff will be here soon."

"Get away from here, Fargo!" Kyle's voice called out, "Don't forget I got a hostage in here. If you try to stop me, she's gonna die."

"I'm coming in, Kyle."

"Don't try it!"

Fargo took a deep breath, then ducked into the doorway, keeping low. There was a shot, and he heard the bullet whiz over his head. He took cover behind a stall.

"Okay, Kyle, I'm in," he said, "and you're not getting out."

"What do you want, Fargo?" Kyle called. "You want the money? Is that it? Here."

Suddenly, the satchel was tossed out into the middle of the stable.

"There's the money. Go ahead and take it."

He was sure the minute he stepped out to grab it Kyle would shoot him.

"I don't want the money, Kyle."

"What do you want then?"

"I want you," Fargo said. "We got your three partners, and I figured out that poor Zack Wheeler was in on the robbery. That leaves you."

"Take the money and go back to Fort Leavenworth, Fargo," Kyle said. "If you don't, somebody's gonna die in here."

"And it might be you."

"It might be me," Kyle said, "and it might be you, but for sure this woman is gonna die."

"I don't think so."

"Why not?"

"You set your other partners up to be killed, Kyle," Fargo said, "but I don't think you want this one dead."

There was no reply.

"I think Karen is the one you were planning on sharing the money with."

After a few moments of silence Karen called out, "Fargo, help me!"

"You've got to sound more convincing that that, Karen," he said.

Some more silence, and then Karen's voice, as he'd never heard it before. "How did you know?"

"How long does it take to get a picnic basket, Karen?" he asked. "Besides, I didn't know for sure until just now, when you told me."

"Damn you, Fargo," she said. "I should have killed you somewhere along the way."

"You couldn't, Karen."

"Why not?"

"We were having too much fun, weren't we?"

No answer.

"Spending nights together on the trail and in hotels. Taking baths together."

"You're a liar!" Sam Kyle shouted.

"How about last night in the hayloft, Karen?" Fargo called. "Did you tell Kyle about that? Did you ever have a night like that with him?"

"I'm gonna kill you, Fargo!" Kyle shouted.

"Has your boyfriend ever cared more about your pleasure than his?"

"Fargo—"

At that moment Sheriff Marc Ryan came running into the stable. "Fargo!"

"Get down!"

But it was too late, Sam Kyle fired, and the sheriff went down.

"First the law, and now you, Fargo," Kyle said.

"Step out and do it like a man, Kyle," Fargo said. "Come on, show your girlfriend what a man you are."

No reply.

"I don't think she's ever seen it, up to now."

"You're a dead man," Kyle said, coming out from his cover.

Fargo stepped out, and the two men squared off.

"Idiots!" he heard Karen shout before they both fired.

Karen looked down at the body of her boyfriend, shaking her head. "Men are such idiots," she said. "There were other ways."

"Not for him," Fargo said.

"Or you, apparently," she said, looking at him. "Does this prove you're a better man than he was?"

"I thought I did that last night."

She studied him for a few moments, then her face softened. "Actually, you did," she said. "In every way you've proven yourself more of a man than he ever was."

"Changing your tune now, Karen?"

"No," she said, "I'm getting smart." She pointed to the satchel, still in the middle of the stable. "There's a lot of money in there, Fargo. Enough for you and me to have fun together for a long time."

"Sorry, Karen."

"Why not?" she asked. "You like me—I know you do."

"I did like you," he said, "before I knew you had a hand in killing those people in the coach."

"Only the judge," she said. "He had a gun of his own, so I had to shoot him myself. Sam and the others took care of the rest."

"And why the charade with me?"

"Because I didn't know Sam was so stupid. I didn't realize he'd left you alive until you found me. I was supposed to be the only one left so I could tell our story, blame the robbery on someone else. Once you and I started out together, I never really had a chance to kill you, did I?" She started to move toward him. "You were right—we were having too much fun."

"Just back off, Karen," Fargo said. "I'm going to check and see how badly the sheriff is hurt. After that

I'll take you over to a cell, with your young friend. You can wait there for the federal marshal."

Fargo walked over to where the sheriff lay and leaned over him. The man's eyes were open, etched with pain. "No trouble up to now, damn you," he said.

Fargo examined the wound in the man's side. "It's not bad. You'll make it. I'll get you to a doctor."

"He's probably drunk."

"Come on, Sheriff," Fargo said, "up you go."

Holding his gun in one hand, he helped the sheriff to his feet with the other. Once they were both standing, he looked over at Karen just as the sheriff yelled, "Look out!"

She had gotten to the satchel, opened it, and taken out the gun that was in there with the money.

"Karen, damn it, don't!" Fargo shouted, but she was beyond hearing him. She brought the gun up, and Fargo had no choice but to shoot her. The bullet hit her in the chest. A look of disbelief came over her face, and then she fell over backward, landing very near her dead boyfriend.

"You could have had her and the money, Fargo," Ryan said. "I couldn't have stopped you. Why didn't you?"

"Wasn't my money, Sheriff," Fargo said, "and she wasn't my woman. It's as simple as that."

LOOKING FORWARD!
The following is the opening
section from the next novel in the exciting
Trailsman **series from Signet:**

THE TRAILSMAN # 205
MOUNTAIN MANKILLERS

1861—the mile-high Rockies, where a fiery mix
of gold and greed proved to be more explosive
than a keg of black powder . . .

The place had an air of danger about it, like a snake
den swarming with rattlers. Or a pool of quicksand
waiting to suck in unwary victims.

The Trailsman stared at the grungy mining camp
from atop a high ridge and did not like what he saw. He
could not say why. The camp was no different from
countless others that had sprung up since word leaked
of gold in the Rockies. Word of the fortunes to be
made, if people were lucky enough. If they survived
the long trek west, the hostiles and the bandits, the heat
and the storms, the drought and widespread disease.
And if, by some miracle, they were one of the rare few
to actually stumble on a rich vein.

Most of those who came wound up dirt poor, or
dead. Yet that had not stopped thousands from flocking

to the mile-high mountains, where many of the stark peaks were crowned year-round with glistening mantles of snow. Gold fever was hard to shake, and more contagious than the measles. Once a man was infected, he might desert his friends, his kin, even his own wife and children, and set off with a crazed gleam in his eyes in search of his personal El Dorado.

Skye Fargo wanted no part of it. He had never been rich and had no real hankering to be. If it happened, it happened. Fine. But he was not about to go mad with gold lust, as so many had. His treasure was the wilderness itself—his treasure and his home. Sparkling stars were the roof over his head at night, his bed always a cushion of soft grass.

Yes, there were perils, but no life was risk free. And having to deal daily with savage beasts and even more savage men had unforeseen benefits. For one thing, it had honed his senses to a razor's edge. He could see a hawk soar a mile off, could hear the whisper of a butterfly's wings. He had few rivals when it came to tracking. And somehow he had acquired a sort of special intuition, a feeling that came over him whenever unseen danger loomed.

Such as now. Fargo's piercing lake-blue eyes narrowed as he studied the mining camp. There was the usual collection of grimy tents and rickety shacks. Plus a few buildings substantial enough to withstand a strong Chinook. Few people were abroad, but it was early yet, only the middle of the afternoon. Most were off along Dew Creek or its tributaries, working their claims. Come nightfall, the gold-crazed legion would return and turn the quiet camp into a raging hell.

Fargo intended to be long gone by then. He was inclined to give the camp a wide berth, but he was in need of a few supplies. With a toss of his head he shook off the feeling of unease and clucked to the Ovaro. He held it to a walk as he descended, his right hand on his thigh close to his Colt. His hat brim was pulled low against the stiff breeze that stirred the whangs on his buckskins.

A crudely painted sign identified the camp. DEW CLAW, Fargo read. He had never heard of it, but that was not unusual. Mining camps had shorter life spans than most moths. They were here today, gone tomorrow. Or as soon as the latest strike played out. Originally, Dew Claw had a population of 210. But someone had crossed that out and written 794 below. Then the 794 had been crossed off, and a new figure, 1431, added. But that last number no longer applied, either. A knife had carved an *X* over it. And at the bottom of the sign, in bold red letters, had been scrawled: Who the hell cares? Fargo could not help but grin.

A few weary horses were tied to makeshift hitch rails. Dirty men in dirtier clothes were everywhere. The street—if it could be dignified by such a grand term—was inches thick in clinging mud. The whole camp was as glum as the cloudy sky overhead.

Several dandies in store-bought clothes stood out like proverbial sore thumbs. Fargo had seen their kind before—human vultures. Those who flocked to wherever gold was found to prey on those who found it.

Those who lined their pockets with the dust and nuggets that rightfully belonged to others. Storekeepers who marked up the cost of goods five hundred percent. Gamblers who had more cards up their sleeves than in their decks. Footpads who would as soon knife a man in the ribs as look at him.

Fargo drew the gaze of everyone he passed. Big and broad-shouldered, he was a tawny panther among half-starved wolves. Some of the stares were merely curious. Others were unfriendly. A large, scruffy man in a bulky coat glanced his way, looked off, then glanced at him again, a hint of recognition dawning.

An empty rail beckoned. Fargo drew rein and started to ease his right foot from the stirrup.

"You can't hitch your animal there, mister."

At the corner of a ramshackle building stood a girl of ten or twelve, all freckles and teeth. Her clothes had been patched up so many times, they appeared as if they had been made from a quilt. Fargo returned her warm smile, then nodded. "This one reserved, is it?" He said it in jest. No one had the right to reserve a hitch rail. First come, first served, was always the general rule.

"Yes, sir," the sprout answered. "Rowdy Joe and his bunch have staked a claim on it. No one else is to tie up here, ever." Dipping a hand into a frayed pocket, she proudly flourished a coin. "He pays me to tell folks to keep away."

The hitch rail was in front of a seedy establishment with the appropriate name of the Timberline Saloon. Bear-hide flaps covered the windows, and the solid wood door was closed. It probably would not be open for business for another couple of hours yet. Fargo shrugged and started to dismount. Whoever had the gall to claim the hitch rail would likely not show up until then. So he had plenty of time to buy the supplies he needed and be on his way.

"Hold on!" the girl declared in alarm. "Didn't you hear me? Rowdy Joe won't take it kindly. Buck him and he'll pound you to a pulp, for certain sure. Honest. I've seen him do it to other folks."

"He won't do it to me," Fargo said matter-of-factly while looping the stallion's reins around the pole. Stretching, he scanned the street. A sizable tent farther down advertised itself as the DEW CLAW MERCANTILE. Fishing fingers into his own pocket, he found an even bigger coin. "Here."

The girl caught it in midair, gaped a moment, then bit it as if to prove it was real. "Golly, mister. A silver dollar. Who do you want me to shoot?"

Fargo chuckled and hooked his thumb into his gun belt. "I want you to watch my horse for me. If anyone lays a hand on him or tries to move him, you're to fetch me right away. I'll be in the general store."

"I'll guard him with my life." She beamed. "I'm Amanda, but most people hereabouts call me Mandy. Maybe you'd like to come over to our claim later and meet my sisters? They're both powerful in need of a handsome feller like you."

"Is that a fact?" Fargo responded, wondering if she meant what he thought she meant. Mining camps attracted fallen doves in droves. Having dallied with more than his share, he was always willing to enjoy their company. But not this time. He had to be in Denver in three days on business.

"Yep, it is," Mandy answered. "They're both getting long in the tooth. Why, Nina is pretty near twenty-two! If she doesn't marry soon, she's afeared she'll end her days a lonely old spinster."

Again Fargo chuckled. "Twenty-two is ancient, all right. But I'm not on the hunt for a wife right now. Tell your sisters not to fret. Sooner or later the right man will come along."

"That's what Pa always said," Mandy replied, her features clouding. "Before we lost him."

"Your father died?"

"Yes, sir. Leastwise, we think he did. No one ever found his body. Just blood." Her voice broke, and her lower lip quivered. "Happened a fortnight ago. Some say a grizzly was to blame. Others say it was Injuns. My sisters think it was—" Mandy stopped, her gaze drifting past him, her eyes widening in sudden fright.

Fargo turned.

Three men approached. Two had the unmistakable stamp of guns for hire. But the third was a strutting peacock dressed in the finest shirt, pants, and shoes money could buy. In his left hand he twirled a polished cane. To everyone he passed, he nodded, as might royalty to peasants. When he spied the Ovaro, he broke stride. His gaze strayed to Fargo, and he smirked. "Well, well. What have we here, Mandy? Someone who wouldn't listen? Didn't you tell him about Rowdy Joe?"

Fargo took an instant dislike to the man. "Ask me, not her," he declared gruffly.

One of the gunmen, a scarecrow whose clawed fingers were hooked to draw, took a step forward but was halted by the peacock's outstretched arm.

"Fair enough, friend. I'm Luke Olinger. I own the Timberline." He said it in the same high-and-mighty fashion the queen of England might say, "I own the Crown Jewels."

"Good for you."

Olinger's smirk evaporated. Resting the cane on his shoulder, he studied Fargo closely. "You're new here, so I'll make allowances. There are a few facts you should learn. First, I pretty much run Dew Claw. Rile me and you'll regret it. Second, Rowdy Joe is a business associate. As much as I despise him, he's not the kind of man to trifle with. So move your horse while you still can."

Fargo never liked being told what to do. Since he had been knee-high to a buffalo calf, he had resented it. His life was his own, to live as he saw fit. Yet another reason he would never settle back East. He enjoyed his freedom too much to ever let politicians, or anyone else, ride roughshod over him. "The pinto stays put."

The scarecrow gun-shark was poised to slap leather. "Just say the word, Mr. Olinger, and I'll move that damn critter. And teach this hombre a lesson, besides."

Olinger was either uncommonly smart or cautious by nature. "Sheathe your claws, Horner. We'll let Rowdy Joe deal with this upstart." The smirk returned, and Olinger twirled his cane. "I must thank you in advance, friend, for the entertainment you will shortly provide. The days are so dull in this flea-ridden pit. I much prefer the excitement and gaiety of St. Louis."

Fargo did not care what the dandy liked. "I'm not your friend." Pivoting, he stalked off, as angry at himself as he was at Olinger and Horner. His temper had gotten the better of him. It would have been a simple matter to tie the stallion to another hitch rail. Was his pride so important he was willing to shed blood over a trifle? The answer was yes! For once a man started backing down, it became a habit. Before he knew it, he was slinking around like a whipped cur, his tail always between his legs. Fargo would be damned if he would ever let that happen to him.

The mercantile was quiet. A couple of middle-aged women were paging through a thick catalogue, daydreaming of luxuries they would never own. Behind the counter stood a gray-haired man with spectacles perched on the end of his nose. He looked up from the ledger he was writing in. "Can I help you?"

Fargo's order was a short one. Coffee, ammunition for his Colt and the Henry, and enough jerky to last until Denver. While waiting, he examined a fancy saddle on a rack. The sign said it was a new three-quarter rig. Recently he had seen its like down El Paso way.

Saddles always interested him. His was one of the best. It had to be. He spent more time on horseback than most men, so his rig had to be comfortable as well as practical. Which was why he'd had his custom-made. Like a Texas rig, it sported two cinches. The tree was slightly longer than most, the cantle slightly wider. The apple was higher and flat-topped for ease in wrapping a rope. And where most riders were content to make do with short skirts, he had asked for a full-square skirt under the tree to reduce wear and chaffing on the Ovaro.

The front flap parted. Fargo shifted, alert for trouble, but it was only a young woman—a lovely young woman with luxurious auburn hair, vivid green eyes, and features as fine as any ever chiseled by the best sculptors who ever lived. Her seedy shirt and pants did not detract in the least from her beauty, nor from the vitality she radiated. Chin high, she marched to the counter and smacked a hand down hard. "Lester Cavendar! What's this Ella tells me about our credit being no good?"

The man with the spectacles was on a ladder, removing a can of Arbuckle's from a shelf. Nervously licking his thin lips, he mustered a smile. "Now, now, Nina. Don't you start in on me. Can I help it if your family has run up such a high bill?"

"Who are you trying to kid?" Nina retorted. "Our bill isn't half as large as some. You've cut us off because you were told to. Fess up."

Lester tried to be stern, but it was like a kitten trying to act fierce. It just couldn't be done. "See here. I own this store, not anyone else. I can do as I see fit. And I say that unless you pay your outstanding debts, I can't grant you any more credit." He sniffed in disdain. "This is a business, woman. Not a charity. You would do well to remember that."

"Is that so?" Placing both hands flat, Nina swung lithely over the counter, then gripped the ladder. "Now *you* see here. How do you expect my sisters and me to get by? Want us to put on dresses and prance around in saloons?"

"How you make your living is not my concern," Lester said testily. "And I'll thank you to move so I can get down."

But Nina did not budge. Instead, she gave the ladder a little shake—just enough to cause Lester to shriek and grab hold of a shelf for support. "We need vittles, consarn it. Some dried beans will do. And flour. And butter if you have any."

"What? No bacon? Or maybe you want me to throw in a side of beef for free?" Cavendar's sarcasm was thick enough to cut with a knife. "You're not getting a thing, and that's final."

"I'm not leaving without it," Nina insisted. She shook the ladder again, violently this time. Lester squawked and clung on for dear life, nearly dropping the coffee. "If it were only Ella and me, I wouldn't make a fuss. But we have Mandy to think of. Do you want her to starve to death just because you don't have any backbone?"

Fargo's interest perked. Mandy was the girl by the saloon. So Nina must be one of her sisters. He moved toward the counter.

Lester had more spine than Fargo had figured. Although scared silly, he glared and snapped, "Your family owes twenty-seven dollars and sixty cents. Until that is paid, my hands are tied. If I were to go easy on you, others would expect the same treatment. Why, I'd be bankrupt in no time."

"Have a heart," Nina pleaded. "You know how rough it's been for us since our pa died. But we're still working the claim. We'll be able to pay you off in a couple of weeks."

"When you do, I will gladly sit down and discuss re-opening your account. Until then, try rabbit stew. I hear tell there are plenty in the woods."

Nina's cheeks flushed scarlet. "I bet you shed your skin once a month, like a snake! Come down from there so I can scratch your eyes out."

"You wouldn't dare!"

Any fool could see that she would. Fargo cleared his throat and announced, "If the lady has no objections, I'll pay her bill."

Both the beauty and the proprietor were momentarily flabbergasted. Lester's mouth moved like that of a fish out of water. It was a full five seconds before he found his voice. "What? Who are you? What business is this of yours? You can't settle their account."

Fargo's temper surged anew. What was it about the business owners in Dew Claw, he wondered, that made them think they had the God-given right to boss others around? "It's up to the lady, not you." Nina was inspecting him as if he had just dropped out of the sky. Touching his hat brim, he said, "I couldn't help but overhear. For your sister's sake, let me help you."

"You know Ella?"

"No. Mandy."

Amazement and something else flitted across Nina's

face. She flushed again, though not from anger. "I appreciate the kindness, mister. I truly do. But we don't take handouts. We're poor, but we don't impose on others. Our pa always told us that we shouldn't be beholden to anyone. So we'll have to decline. Sorry."

"There are no strings attached," Fargo assured her. "If you want, repay me when you and your sisters are back on your feet. Send the money care of the sutler's at Fort Laramie. He's a friend of mine."

"We just couldn't," Nina said, but she was plainly tempted.

"I didn't see one rabbit on the way in," Fargo mentioned. "And I'd hate for Mandy to go hungry because you're too stubborn for your own good."

Nina pursed her mouth. A mouth, Fargo noted, shaped like a ripe strawberry. Her homespun shirt swelled nicely in front, while her thighs were as exquisitely shaped as any he had ever seen. "Are you sure you have the money to spare?" she asked.

Fargo nodded. Just barely. Subtracting the cost of his own provisions, he'd have about two bucks left to his name. Not much, but when he arrived in Denver, he was due to collect a couple of hundred. He made a show of counting out the twenty-seven dollars and sixty cents.

Lester had descended. Anyone could tell part of him did not want to take the money, and part of him did. Greed won. Scooping it up, he fondled it as a man might a lover. "Consider the sisters all paid up."

"You'll extend them a new line of credit," Fargo said.

The merchant looked at him and opened his mouth as if to object. But something he saw in Fargo's expression changed his mind. "Whatever you say, stranger. I reckon I'm just a generous soul."

"In a pig's eye," Nina muttered. Her green eyes fixed on her tall benefactor and for a fleeting instant betrayed deep gratitude. "I can't thank you enough. We haven't had a decent meal in days. All the money we had disappeared when our pa died. Since then we've been living hand to mouth."

"Glad I can help."

Lester did not know when to leave well enough alone. Snickering, he leaned on an elbow and quipped, "What are you, mister? A Good Samaritan? Or were you hoping to get in this uppity filly's britches?"

Fargo's right hand shot out. His fingers clamped on the owner's throat, clamped tight, and squeezed. Lester grabbed his wrist and pulled and pushed. But the man had the strength of a day-old infant. Fargo shook him as a lynx might shake a rodent. "Not all jackasses have four legs, Cavendar. Savvy?"

Terror-stricken, the proprietor whined.

"I'll be back this way one day. I'd hate to hear that you've mistreated Nina or her sisters. If you agree to behave yourself, blink twice."

Sputtering and wheezing, Lester frantically fluttered his eyelids eight or nine times.

Still squeezing, Fargo smiled at the beauty. "See? Most people will be as polite as can be if you only take the time to explain things to them." He shoved, slamming Cavendar against the shelves with such force they swayed and threatened to topple. "Now, if you'll excuse me, ma'am. I have a lot of hard riding to do before nightfall." Collecting his supplies, Fargo plunked payment down and departed.

Lester never uttered another peep. Doubled over, beet red, he sucked in air like a bellows gone amok. If looks could kill, though, he'd have shriveled Fargo down to the size of an ant just to squish him underfoot.

"Wait, mister!"

Fargo was almost out through the flap. He'd had a bellyful of Dew Claw. It was a hellhole, a festering den of sidewinders and polecats, just like dozens of other camps he had come across in his travels. Anyone who stayed there was asking for grief. The sooner he was shed of the place, the happier he would be.

"You never told me your handle."

"Skye Fargo." Assuming that was the end of it, he left. He should have known better. She tagged along, chattering like an excited chipmunk.

"Can I call you Skye? I wish you weren't in such an all-fired hurry to leave. Ella and I would be right pleased if you'd come have supper with us. She's a wonderful cook. Her biscuits will melt in your mouth. And her coffee is the best this side of the Mississippi. Pa said so himself many a time."

"Mandy told me he disappeared. Have any idea of what happened to him?"

"You bet I do!" Nina was going to say more, but a commotion up the street gave her pause.

A small crowd had gathered in front of the Timberline Saloon. Four men on horseback were also there, close to the hitch rail. A high-pitched voice cried out and was greeted by harsh laughter. Fargo quickened his pace, his gut balling into a knot. He had a fair inkling of what he would find, and shouldering through the spectators, he learned his hunch was right. Mandy had hold of the Ovaro's reins and was trying to keep a husky bull of a man from seizing them. She was scared, but trying not to show it.

"Please, Mr. Guthrie! A man paid me to watch over this animal!"

The human bull made a grab at her, but Mandy skipped aside, provoking more mirth. Hemmed in as she was, she could not go more than a few feet in any direction. Adding to the poor girl's woes, the Ovaro nickered and bobbed its head, nearly jerking her off balance.

"Try harder, Rowdy Joe!" an onlooker hollered.

"Maybe you should pick on someone smaller," hooted another. "This one is a regular wildcat!"

"She's more than you can handle!" chimed in a third.

Rowdy Joe Guthrie was not amused. His head was as broad as a longhorn's, his forehead as high, and slanted. He had oversized ears that resembled shorn horns, ears his wide-brimmed brown hat could not quite hide. An ill-fitting brown shirt covered his barrel chest. His pants were black. Brawny, callused hands opened and clenched in irritation as he took a short step and bellowed, "Enough of your shenanigans, girl! Give me the reins and I'll forget how you've bucked me."

Mandy was on the verge of tears. "Please! I don't want to make you mad! But I can't let you beat him any more!"

That was when Fargo saw the cottonwood switch in Rowdy Joe's left hand and the welt on the pinto's neck. He shook from head to toe, as if cold, but what he felt was fiery inner heat. A red haze seemed to shroud the whole world. Dimly, he was conscious of turning, of shoving the coffee and the ammunition and the jerky into startled Nina's arms. Then his legs were moving of their own accord. His left hand fell on Rowdy Joe's shoulder and spun Guthrie around. His right hand, balled into an iron fist, swept up in a vicious arc, his knuckles smashing full into the bigger man's jaw.

The blow would have felled a lesser foe. Teeth crunched, scarlet drops spattered every which way, and Rowdy Joe tottered back against the hitch rail. The cottonwood switch dropped, but Joe did not. Stunned silence gripped the crowd as he snorted, spat blood, then glowered at the Trailsman.

Mandy whooped for joy. "You're back! Thank goodness! I didn't know how much longer I could hold him off!"

Rowdy Joe Guthrie straightened. "So this is your cayuse, is it?"

In the doorway of the saloon someone chortled. Luke Olinger stepped from the shadows, leaned on the jamb, and tapped the wood with the ivory knob on the end of his cane. "Your brilliance never fails to astound me, Joseph. I'm dying to know whether you can count to twelve without taking off your boots." The dandy jabbed the cane in Fargo's direction. "Who else would he be? There isn't another living soul in all of Dew Claw with enough grit to stand up to you."

"Don't use that tone on me," Rowdy Joe warned. "Not unless you want your teeth kicked down your throat."

Luke shook his head and sighed. "Typical. You threaten me, when the curly wolf in front of you is the one you should be venting your spleen on. Or could it be that you're afraid of him?"

"I'm not afraid of anyone or anything!" Rowdy Joe declared. And with that, he lowered his head, extended both arms, and charged Fargo.